PRAISE FOR FIRE

M000286576

In *Fires*, Murray Dunlap slaloms between nonfiction accounts of the accident that changed his life and works of pure invention, short stories and flash fiction pieces, many of which were written before the accident. Not only does this blending of fact and fiction make for good reading, plain and simple, but it also presents us with a privileged glimpse of a man in flux, before and after, how he has changed, how he has remained the same, how he's still finding his way. Ultimately, this book will make readers bottomlessly glad that he survived his metaphorical fire–wounded, yes, but wiser and still writing.

Michael Knight, celebrated author of *The Typist, Divining Rod, Goodnight, Nobody,* and *Dogfight and Other Stories.*

Murray Dunlap's stories crackle with originality and craft. Along with his compelling personal story, Dunlap offers inventive glimpses into the meaning of identity and the power that past losses hold over us. His writing is by turns funny and nostalgic, with memorable sentences that radiate with wisdom and insight. Fires and Other Stories burns with the white-hot light of an impressive talent.

Kirk Curnutt, author of *Raising Aphrodite, Dixie Noir,* and *Breathing Out the Ghost*

Murray Dunlap is that rare writer with the ability to step outside himself "to familiarize the strange and mystify the familiar." Readers will celebrate that this clever, perceptive, earthy writer survived both physically and emotionally to rise like the iconic phoenix from a fiery wreckage in order to "type on" and give us the gift of his thoughts and stories.

Tara L. Masih
Author of *Where the Dog Star Never Glows: Stories*
Editor of *The Rose Metal Press Field Guide to Writing Flash Fiction*
Series Editor, *The Best Small Fictions*

When you read Dunlap's stories, you can feel the landscape springing up around you —the cypress roots and pine needles, the weight of the air and the pull of the water. The landscape is deeply tied to the idea of home, and there's a weight to that, too, whether characters are being driven away from it or dragged back to it. Or both. Dunlap himself is more than one of these dragged and driven characters. He is the Murray Dunlap before his life-changing car wreck, and he is the Murray Dunlap after it. Writing about his continued recovery, he sifts and sorts through possible choices, possible selves, always seeking. These stories make the reader glad that he keeps on searching."

Gin Phillips, author of *The Well and the Mine* and *Come in and Cover Me*

We can choose to look at Murray as the poor writer who suffered a traumatic brain injury. We can choose to look at him as someone who lost the kind of life it could kill a person to lose. Or we can choose to look at him as a writer who went through some shit and now has another story to tell.

Kristen Tsetsi, former reporter for *The Journal Inquirer* and contributor to the video series, *Inside the Writers' Studio.*

FIRES
AND OTHER STORIES

Stories of unexpected turns in life,
including one man's fight to start entirely over

For Elizabeth! Enjoy!

Murray Dunlap

The Ardent Writer Press, LLC
Brownsboro, Alabama

Visit Murray Dunlap's Author Page at

www.ArdentWriterPress.com

For general information about publishing with The Ardent Writer Press contact *steve@ardentwriterpress.com* or forward mail to: The Ardent Writer Press, Box 25, Brownsboro, Alabama 35741.

ISBN 978-1-938667-36-7

Library of Congress Control Number: 2015934754
Library of Congress subject headings:
- •Short stories, American--Alabama.
- •Short stories.
- •Short stories, American.
- •Short stories, American--Southern States.
- •Short story and poetry collection.

First Edition

CONTENTS
FIRES AND OTHER STORIES

DEFIANCE	8
OTHERWISE	10
PUT IT RIGHT	13
TIMING	16
ACROSS THE PADDOCK	19
HIGHWAY 50	23
TALK ABOUT GOD	25
CALDER'S BIG SEXY FULCRUM	30
THE PHILOSOPHY OF RUNNING	39
RED LIGHT (A FIRE OF ITS OWN)	42
THE BURIAL OF THE DEAD	47
PAPA, I AM ABOUT TO SAIL	52
THE RIVER	55
A HAPPY ENDING	57
FIRES	61

TAUROMAQUIA 84

TREASURE 95

DOG DECISION 104

FOUR DAY WORRY BLUES 110

LOVE 122

SEIZURE 123

OUR ROUTINE 125

TIMES I NEARLY DIED 129

LAST WILL AND TESTAMENT 133

RUNNING MULE HOLLOW 137

BUDDY 146

NEIGHBORS 154

FEIGNING NONCHALANCE 161

FORCES OF NATURE 164

AUTHOR'S NOTE -
FROM PAIN AND SUFFERING TO JOY 166

Defiance - Murray Dunlap

In defiance of depression, I lift my chin, and I smile.
Our lives take unexpected turns, always.
Some sharper than others.
On a dime, my life turned inside out.
I was confused, angry, and thought of ending my life.
But, in defiance of depression, I have moved on to smile.
When I lift my chin to kiss my love, I am reminded: So very much to embrace.
And so many things to love. Life is good, after all. In spite of it all.
With the God-given grace to start over, I do just that.
The coma: I woke up.
The wheelchair: I stood up.
The book: I wrote.
With a fire in my belly, I turn to face the world.
I turn in defiance of depression, and I remember to smile.

Published by the *Cahaba River Literary Journal*

FIRES

And Other Stories

Kara Swanson says, "The curious thing about the auto accident that ended my life was that I lived through it."

Again, for my mother and brother.

When I was forced to pull myself out of a deep, dark hole, I thank Dr. Tom Davis (Athens) and Dr. Melissa Ogden (Mobile), who both showed me where to climb… (and who are putting themselves out of business by healing so quickly).

OTHERWISE...

"From the gutter-most to the utter-most."
– Garrett Williamson about Murray Dunlap's recovery
on WKRG news interview.

IT STARTED AS THE PERFECT MARRIAGE. Two young, attractive, kind-hearted people... And then the wreck. A man failed to look up to see a red-light and so he hit this kid straight-on in the passenger side door. Thank God, there were no passengers. So he was crushed in a wreck, being pushed into a truck full of friends of all things. They turned out fine, but this kid, me, was sent into a three month coma. And that wreck, on 6-7-08, marked the beginning of the end of this perfect marriage. The actual end was on September 10th, 9-10. So if numbers are your thing, those are pretty clear bookmarks. And so, our divorce is final. The perfect marriage, up in flames.

The worst part is that we have yet to have a fight. Not once.

That said, and we are in agreement on this one thing: I am a different man post-wreck. After three months of coma and six months in a wheelchair, I'm not sure anyone would be the same. I'm going to walk again, and I've already made the switch to using a walker. That said, I sure could use a good long jog. But no. No jogging for me. Not now. And because I have a Traumatic-Brain-Injury, I have no balance. If I even try to walk without something to hold onto, I fall flat on my face.

And so, as a pre-wreck marathon running perfectionist, my ex-wife mourns the loss of her husband. Literally. And who knows who I am now…

I also never sleep anymore. And I've tried sleep-aid medicine, but get this: Traumatic-Brain-Injuries are tricky things. So being extremely sleep deprived, I had the generic of Ambien called in for me. But due to the brain, it made me sleep-walk. So, not only was I using a walker, my brain decided for me to get on up at 3 a.m. I put shoes on and everything. And in my state of sleep, I never thought to use the walker. Nope. So after one step, I fell to my right knee and sprained my ankle. I also rocked forward and hit my forehead hard enough to get a bruised cut.

So this could have easily ended in a mortuary. But I press on. And I smile. At this point, I have to. I'm not dead yet. And whenever anyone hears my story, they are quick to commend me for pressing on. But all I can think is – What choice do I have?

Why keep going? Because I can. And it is clear that I have no other options… Having been very nearly killed in a ridiculous car wreck last year, I do whatever I am capable of. Spending three months in a coma, followed by six months in a wheelchair will do that to you. As you read this, I'm out of the wheelchair, but a Traumatic-Brain-Injury caused my brain to stop talking to my legs, so I´m still using a walker. Sadly. Many months later.

So I sat in that chair for the full recovery term just itching to get out and do something. Anything. I had gone jogging for 15 miles just an hour before the wreck. Obviously, when I was in the wheelchair, I was NOT happy. In the walker, I´m just angry. So I go to therapy five days a week and hope like hell it will work. It seems to be – the switch from the wheelchair to the walker made this obvious - but SO slowly.

And then, Liam Neeson's wife was all over the news for having died of exactly what I have. A Traumatic-Brain-Injury. But I don't give up. I couldn't imagine just giving in and being fine with being paralyzed. I now have infinitely more respect for the lives of the handicapped! It is an amazing thing at 35 years of age to be faced with an entire life in front of you, but in a much, MUCH more limited way.

So now I'm planning to run marathons again. I'm not nearly there yet, but I'm determined, and anyone who knows me knows that that's all it takes to be sure I'll do something. Determined, yes. Crazy, no. And whatever drove the pre-wreck man to run five marathons is clearly driving me to run again. Who knows why? I'm simply determined and that is all I know.

Now one more set of weightless squats. The movement is like that of a weight lifter, but no weights. The idea being I'll improve my balance and leg strength. I hope so. Having no job to go to, and being so lonely, I do these over and over again.

So divorce? Yes. Suicide? No. I have no idea what motivates me. Why don't I give up entirely? I guess I'm just determined to defeat the odds stacked against me.

And I'm angry. The fact that a man I've never met failed to pay attention for one single second of his entire life and now I'm divorced, trying to relearn to walk at 35, and not sure what the hell I'm doing – really - it seems to me that anger is the consistent motivator. I flat out refuse to let one man failing to pay attention for one half-second ruin my entire life. I'm crawling with anger just saying that.

Sigh.

And my ex-wife and I will go to dinner tonight as friends. Can you imagine? The strange thing is that we still care about each other very much. I'm just different, she says. I don't really see how, but oh-well. She is entitled to her opinion. With a fractured brain, who am I to say otherwise?

PUT IT RIGHT

*For Bob and Ellen Gentle, and everyone in Fairhope, Alabama
(especially at Panini Pete's) who helped me put it right.*

THE EASY THING TO DO was to take the little bits of clarity from Rob's slurry words and nod and move along. His slur was from medication, not alcohol – as some would assume, and Rob was very self-conscious about the way he sounded. He desperately wanted to go back in time to a day when he had felt confident in his voice.

The hard part came when anyone tried to make sense of him, or worse, to ask him what he meant. And that is when the trouble started for a girl named Joy and when everything turned into a cloud of confused anger. That, of course, is where our story begins.

What Joy had done was ask Rob, "What do you mean when you say *balance*?"

And Rob said nothing. His personal balance had been ruined by a car wreck, never to be regained. He also could no longer drive. Painfully, Rob made his way through life. Not working at a regular job like everyone else, not standing with any certainty, not doing anything really, save for his carpentry. He used his workshop as a release and a valuable tool. He used it to pay his way.

Finally, he turned to Joy and gave an answer. "I mean like you standing there. You know. Certain everything is where it is and nothing will move suddenly," Rob said. "It's like that if you then were to carbonate your brain and shake it up."

"But you seem to be standing fine," Joy started reluctantly.

"Yes," Rob replied. "But watch this."

At which time Rob turned and used his head swing as if he was looking over his shoulder. At which time, he grabbed a hold of the table saw next to him and just barely prevented himself from falling.

"Really?" Joy asked incredulously. "That little movement and all balance is gone?"

"Afraid so," Rob replied. "Or less."

And it became clear to Joy just how fragile Rob had become. All due to a car wreck. One man's failure to glance up and see a red light. It was unbelievable really. This proved to Joy the unjust nature of the world and left her questioning everything, even religion. But Rob's woodwork had taken a brisk turn for the better, so she did not know what to think.

What was, in fact, open and honest for Joy was the precarious nature of Rob's current existence.

Rob sanded the top of a desktop-in-progress. It gave him satisfaction to finish things neatly now that his life was such a mess. He carved out the corners of the desktop and left room for a screw to thread through. He found that creating a puzzle out of his crafts gave him an end to work for, and –for now- it was enough to steer him clear of suicide. And the money he made from selling the finished pieces gave him enough to live on. A magazine had run a story on Rob and sales had doubled. The brisk turn for the better was big.

That said, it was a daily challenge for Rob to keep going. His mind would wander to the ease of the big sleep. No more struggle, no more fighting. The thing that kept him going, of course, is to see what would happen next.

Joy turned to face Rob, who had turned around, but now straightened out and faced Joy once again. And Joy could see that look in Rob of utter frustration. Utter exhaustion.

Rob took the time to look Joy in the eye and say very slowly, and very clearly, "Just one more corner, one more element of design, and I will finish this for my client. For another month, my rent will be paid." Rob said this carefully and with only a hint of slur.

But, all things considered, Joy was happy to see Rob turn and sand the corner of the desktop. His now very-well-selling work. Joy could see the great satisfaction Rob took in adjusting the desktop-in-progress just so. And put things right.

TIMING

THE THEN TINY CHARLES BENNETT PORTER JR. crouched at the spine of the door, peering through the crack that allowed a partial view of my tall and muscular father as he meticulously polished the bow of a one-man sailboat with a chamois cloth. My father, Charles senior, designed the boat himself. He manufactured it in wood to moderate interest. But then came fiberglass and, boom, just like that, they were snapped up by the hundreds all over the Gulf Coast. Then the thousands. Then worldwide. At fifty years of age, my father sold his sailboat company to an international sporting goods corporation for twenty five million dollars. The then tiny Bennett was seven years old.

But two decades spent barking orders in warehouses filled with invisible clouds of fiberglass had seeded my father's lungs with cancer. He coughed blood into the chamois. Charles senior would die quickly. My drunk-driving mother was already dead.

I crouched at the spine of the door, peering at my tall and muscular father. The family dog, a liver Mastiff named Tank, sat at his heel. I was not allowed in the workshop. I was not allowed to play with the tools. Hundreds of gleaming devices tempting me, washing away my mindfulness with the ease of a hypnotist's watch. I had given in once, taking a simple scraper and pretending it was Excalibur. I sliced the air and pronounced myself king.

Charles senior took the then tiny Bennett by the wrist and snatched the scraper from his hand, breaking an index finger and spraining a thumb.

Charles said, "Worthless. Just like your mother. If only you'd been in the car that day. Then I wouldn't have to put up with this shit. You timed your birth all wrong. You got here as I was going sour. You never witnessed me as a great man."

On the drive to the emergency room he said, "I should leave my fortune to the dog. Tank understands obedience. He knows how to behave. It's all a crap shoot anyway."

I crouched at the spine of the door, wishing my tall and muscular father was dead. In less than a year, this would be true. My father gripped his very smooth, very angular chin between a finger and thumb. He leaned in close, eyeing the hull. He rubbed the chamois harder.

I crouched at the spine of the door, seven years old, missing my mother and blaming my father. My twin sister Eleanor was a shadow. A ghost. She quietly appeared and disappeared from rooms, scribbling in her diary with delicate hands. When she left home for an all girls' boarding school, it went entirely unnoticed. But then, how could I know if it was any different for me?

I had imagined my life with a gleaming sword and a white horse. An impenetrable suit of armor. Not the boarding schools and demerits and paddles to come. I did not imagine Yale, nor did I imagine being kicked out. I did not imagine finishing school at the University of Alabama, starting a life in real estate, or falling in with dishonest developers and sour deals. I did not imagine Eleanor's wedding or the shock of her new, self-assured personality that bloomed with love.

I did not imagine my life in a waterfront mansion bought with inherited money. Nor did I imagine two wives, a mistress, five scattered children, glasses of whiskey in shaking hands, and skin surely turning yellow. I did not imagine losing touch with all of my childhood friends. I did not imagine weeklong blackouts, DT's, or the ridiculous, useless interventions. I did not imagine the shame.

Instead, I thought about how the shape of a certain tool, in this case a handheld power saw, seemed to contain magical qualities. That the shape and size and the terrible beauty of sharpened metal made an inanimate object somehow come to life. I desperately longed to touch each tool. I imagined handling them all, conjuring their secrets and unlocking hidden spells. I imagined a line of socket wrenches beginning to march like toy soldiers. I imagined table saws humming as a line of teak planks floated across the blade, hammers and nails taking flight with hummingbird wings and swirling about the room. The tools would work in concert, assembling a sailboat of perfect proportions. I imagined my life as a master craftsman, no -an artist, whose magical boats would be revered, exponentially beyond my fathers.'

After Charles died, the then tiny Bennett stepped the workshop. He beelined for the handheld powersaw, plugged it in, and promptly cut off the top half of his pinky finger. Little Bennett could not have imagined the boundless trajectory of this omen.

I could not have imagined that I would die without love. I supposed I timed that all wrong as well. My father would have moaned about my lack of grace. Of course, he would have moaned about everything, including my sadly lived life.

ACROSS THE PADDOCK

MISS CONKLIN'S FARM sits in a wedge of land on the outskirts of Mobile, Alabama. The manor house lies in the shade of a towering sweet gum. The summer is hot. Her horse, a Hanoverian named Shiloh, defended and lost his title at the 1889 Bit & Spur Races. He braked in front of the rails and the rider flipped out of the saddle. Shiloh snapped the man's spine with a hoof. It's been just over a year since the accident. Today, Shiloh trots across the paddock to see a maiden mare in the neighboring field. Miss Conklin won't race him again; she's put him out to stud.

Ben sits on the wide pine floor boards of the front porch with his hands gripped tight under skinny legs. He sits Indian style and rocks. Beside him, pages curl at the corners of a leather bound notebook. Most of the pages have been written on, top to bottom, with fine blue ink. The letters sit at a backward slant in careful print. A leather strap loops the notebook twice and ends with a secure knot. Miss Conklin pats the bun of blonde hair pinned to her head. She faces the front pasture but sees nothing. Cataracts scar her eyes.

"Are you sure?"

"I'm sure."

"You could go back and look again?"

"I've looked plenty."

"What about under the run-in shed?"

"Yes, ma'am."

"And the water trough?"

"Yes, ma'am, I've looked there too." Ben lifts his arm to show his sleeve is wet. Then he remembers and puts it down.

Gideon Lester waves from the paddock fence marking the property line.

"Mr. Lester is waving at you," he says.

"He knows I'm blind."

"Maybe he's waving to me?"

Ben darts across the yard, keeping his distance from Shiloh. He knows about the accident. He stands on the low beam of the fence.

"Have you seen my blue pen?"

"Sorry, Ben. I ain't seen it."

"What about Mrs. Lester?"

"I reckon she'd a told me if she'd seen it." Gideon wipes his forehead with the hem of his dirty shirt. "How's Miss Conklin gettin' on?"

"She's fine. It's a blue pen with gold trim. I have a notebook too. They go together."

"Sounds like a humdinger, but I ain't seen it."

"Yeah." He looks back to the house. "Goodbye, Mr. Lester."

"See ya, little man."

Ben runs back and sits down on the porch.

"Mr. Lester hasn't seen it either."

"How is Mr. Lester? How did he look?"

"He was sweating pretty good."

Miss Conklin smooths her apron, smiles, then waves in the direction of the fence.

"He's got his back to us now."

She stops waving. A breeze moves through the sweet gum, rustling the leaves.

"Have you looked under Wrigley? You always sit under Wrigley when you write."

"Yes, ma'am, I looked there first."

"Your Daddy gave it to you."

"Yes."

"When did you see him last?"

"Christmastime."

"Same as last year."

"Yes, ma'am."

"Well, you'll have to get another."

"I don't have money. Momma says use a chunk of coal."

"Lord." She pauses. "I wish your Momma could find somebody."
Ben says nothing. "Wait here."

Miss Conklin steps into the house. For the first time in years, she forgets to ease the screen door closed and it bangs against the frame. Shiloh throws his head over the fence and nuzzles the mare.

In the bedroom, Miss Conklin can still smell Mr. Lester among the twisted sheets. She makes the bed quickly, then sits at the vanity. From a drawer, she removes a change purse and feels out a number of coins. She replaces the purse. From the same drawer, she lifts a plaster face, the image of her dead son, and gently sets it down on the maple veneer. Usually, the Reverend embeds the death masks directly into the gravestone with concrete. Erebus Cemetery is filled with them. For Miss Conklin, he made a duplicate in plaster. She glides her fingertips over the smooth white surface every night. Today, she places her hands over the eyes, just for a moment. Then she palms the coins and leaves the room.

Ben feels a tear coming on and wipes it away with the back of his right hand. His left hand drums against the top of the notebook. Miss Conklin reemerges through the screen door and feels her way along the railing until sensing where he sits. The door bangs against the frame. She retrieves the coins from the pocket of her apron and holds them out. Ben does not stand. He lifts his hand to meet hers, brushing against thick, callused fingers.

He takes the coins.

Miss Conklin faces the fence line as if she might see something. She smooths her apron.

"Well, go on."

"Thank you, ma'am."

He grabs the railing and pulls himself to his feet. He tucks the notebook under his left arm.

"Thank you, ma'am."

"All right. Now go on."

Ben jumps down the front steps all at once and runs straight out the drive. The rocks sting his bare feet, and when his hands begin to sweat, he worries he might drop the coins. He shoves them in his pocket.

HIGHWAY 50

TWO A.M. HIGHWAY 50. ELY, NEVADA. We laughed out loud at the Break-a-Heart Hotel in Silver Springs, flew past the Last Chance Saloon in Austin, then passed up the Parsonage House in Eureka. A coyote darted across both lanes a few minutes ago, and I've seen more road-kill in one night than in a lifetime of driving. We're low on gas. From here, the next decent stop is Delta, Utah, and that's one hundred and fifty three miles up the road. I've got a job in Denver to get to, but we won't make it tonight.

Ely it is.

The Prospector is full. So are the Park-Vue and the Copper Queen. Hotel Nevada is no different, so I ask where else we should look. Jessie stays in the car with the doors locked. The girl behind the desk looks to be in her late teens. Her name tag reads: Rose Ellen. She's wearing a red tank top with black bra straps showing and her breasts are so large, they move papers around on the countertop while she talks. This is her job.

"The Jailhouse Motel, I guess," she says. "They always have a room left."

"It ain't the best," I say. "But anything would be fine. Can you call them for us?"

"Sure, baby." Rose shouts into a dark room over her shoulder where the blue light of a television blinks against an obese man's face. "Get up, Bull. What's the number for Lola at Jailhouse?"

Bull opens his eyes, scowls, and turns to Rose. "Look it up, bitch." Bull shakes his face, loose fat jiggling in his cheeks. "Jailhouse?" With considerable effort, Bull stands up. Dark wiry bangs stick to his forehead and a long jagged scar travels the length of his chin. He walks into the doorway, filling it, and looks me in the eye. "You're not going to stay there, are you?"

"Everything is full," I say.

"You feeling lucky?"

"Not especially."

"I wouldn't go to Jailhouse without a bucket of Clorox and a body condom," Bull says. Then he laughs from somewhere deep in his throat.

Rose dials the number and twirls her hair. "Lola," she says. "You got more rooms open? I got a pretty little couple here needs a rest." She pauses and licks her finger. "All right then. I'll send them to you."

I walk back to Jessie, hoping the job in Denver will give us a better life. I jingle the change in my pocket and wonder how cold it will be tonight, sleeping in the car.

TALK ABOUT GOD

For Mary Balfour, with so very much love...

"Above all, keep loving one another earnestly,
since love covers a multitude of sins."
(1 Peter 4:8)

MAC SCRATCHED BEHIND HIS EAR, looked skyward, and said, "OK, so this is how I see it: Our universe in a fish tank. Our species like a fish. Jesus was a fish sent to learn, then send back info about us to God. And as a 'fish' he had to learn about our entire experience, including pain and suffering. Thus his crucification. Make sense?" He leaned back and seemed to allow the plaid chair cushion to envelope him.

Jill leaned back herself and wrung her hands... "I don't know Mac. Are we fish?"

"In my metaphor, yes."

"But clearly not in real life. Do I look like I have gills?"

"You are missing the point, Jill. If God is a scientist of sorts, and keeps our universe in a fish tank, then yes, we are fish. And with that haircut, you might have had gills all along."

"Mac, I'm not feeling this. I am not, nor do I want to be, a fish. Metaphorical or not."

"OK, Jill. Forget it. I was just trying to explain Jesus in a way that made sense to me."

"Ok, ok, ok. God is 'keeping' us in a fish tank so he can watch and help us, right? He can watch over us like a parent."

"Now you are getting my point, Jill. Thank you for playing along."

"But at some point we really have to talk about the baby." Mac stared at Jill in earnest.

"Little Mac just wasn't meant for this world, and we weren't ready." Jill used the back of her hand to wipe her eyes. "Neuroblastoma is one of those rare things. It just is." Jill sucked in a deep breath all at once and looked up with hopeful eyes.

"Rare. But my God, I miss him just the same."

"Radiation usually works well against neuroblastoma. But it spread to so many places in Mac's body…"

"Mac never had a chance. We simply have to know he tried and gave that cancer all he had."

"Mac junior would sit here smiling and doing that funny thing with his little hands if he could. Just know that, love. I swear, to me, he looked like a little Einstein having an 'ah-ha' moment." Big Mac drew his hands into fists.

"If only I had not been smoking in those early days…" Jill looked up with tears in her eyes. "Oh, smokers guilt will kill me yet."

"Jill, the doctor explained to us that had nothing to do with it. He did not know what caused the changes in Mac's body that led to his disease. It's not clear what it was. It just was, Jill."

"If it had anything to do with my stealing smoke breaks, I would just have to die."

"It had nothing to do with that. And if you died, we couldn't try again, now could we?"

"You are right, love. Of course you are right." Jill was happy with this response and leaned back, allowing her hair to float just over her shoulders. Her ready-for-baby-haircut was still an adjustment for Mac. Even 3 months later, the girl he had been in love with since they were teenagers looked so different, it stopped him.

***

MAC WALKED BACK IN to the cabin where they had found themselves staying for the 4th of July. Monteagle Tennessee. The

Assembly. The Assembly is essentially a neighborhood in the woods on top of a mountain, sitting next to Sewanee, the University of the South. Professors and anyone connected to the seminary. All nestled together in the woods with idyllic trails connecting everyone. They have playtime activities for children on Saturdays and they have their own church for Sundays.

"How many times can you walk around over and over the bridges for no reason?"

"It clears my head to walk around, Jill."

"Do you even like it here?"

"My family has been coming here for generations. And yes, I think it is lovely."

"Ok. Just checking on you, love."

"And to answer your earlier question, yes, I am a Christian. I can get behind this now, because I thought about it the whole time I was out walking, and I'm not even sure 'son' is the word we should use... But, I do see how God would create a human, and that this human would need to experience the entire human experience. Even pain and death. And I would guess that Jesus married and had kids too, because like my fish tank analogy, if God put a goldfish in to learn about fishy ways, then sure, that goldfish would find a mate and have baby fishies - as to understand the entire goldfish experience. And then the goldfish would get algae or whatever happens, and suffer and die (his cross)..."

"Heavy. Mac, did you find something to smoke on your walk?"

"So maybe even Jesus was just a part of God's brain, as a learning tool.... So God would understand our algae (or whatever happened to be hurting/killing us) and how it felt. So Jesus maybe was just the back of God's brain, trying to understand his fishies... you know?"

"Now you are seriously talking on weed."

"Jill, I have not, and will not, be smoking weed. I walk to clear my head. Knock the cobwebs loose."

"So it's just us fishies, right Mac? No intellectual enhancement at all. Are you certain you haven't found something out there?"

"Nothing but clean air. And maybe a bit of quiet from the family noise."

"To quiet that, just get me pregnant again."

"Do we want to try again?"

"I don't know if we are ready. Try again: yes. But already?"

"It has been 3 months since we lost little Mac. I got that raise. Our time for a little fishy, if there ever was one, is now."

***

"ARE YOU OK, MAC? You seem a million miles away."

"I woke at 4:30 a.m. today, and lay there thinking about it, and thought of a resurrection analogy that works for me: If scientists have a camera with a microphone out in the field, then even after the experiment is over, they collect the camera/mic and have it to study. Even after the live feed is done. So God needed to bring Jesus back to talk/study, and get the scoop on his fishies."

"The fish! Mac, these fish are killing me!"

"Just deal with it, Jill. I am making a point."

"So, what is your point?"

"Jesus is the conduit for religious love and forgiveness."

"What in Samhill has that got to do with fish?"

"The metaphorical sense of how we deal with each other, and how God, in the end, saves us. And how Jesus gave him all of the information he needed to deal with our complicated species."

"I still think you found a weed you could smoke on your walk."

"I can't lie, Jill. I am a complicated man. If I could change it, I would. But I have set out to understand what it is that makes religion so important and graceful."

"Mac. You are a complicated man who I have chosen to spend the rest of my life with. I love your complications. That said, it does not change my theory that you have found something to smoke on your walks. You go out and come back deeper in thought than is healthy."

"Uh huh…"

"But I love you, Mac."

"And I love you, Jill."

"Hey, love, let's go for a walk and talk about baby names."

"Yes." Mac said. "We are ready."

"Our love can survive this. Our love is strong." Jill grabbed Mac's hand and they started for the door.

This time the pair went for a walk on the grounds of the Assembly together. Mac proved that there was no weed, and Jill proved that she could love a complicated man. And so they loved one another, the complications of a lost baby and all. For the next hour, they planned how they would raise a fish, with a little help from God.

CALDER'S BIG SEXY FULCRUM

Fulcrum:

1. the pivot about which a lever turns
2. something that supports or sustains; prop

THIS STORY MUST BEGIN WITH I, myself that is, Murray Dunlap, the writer of these words —not to be confused with a metanarrative "I," which would signify another layer of the fiction, even if *that* writer names himself, first and last name, but intends no such reality other than an enhancement of his intellectual prose- and you, Michael Knight , the reader of these words —not to be confused with the "you" of second person metanarrative in which the writer intends to address an unspecified "you," an all encompassing "you," or even an "anaden," with the hope of drawing his reader into the prose and engage more deeply. No, in this story, "I" will be me, and "you" will be you.

And I, Murray Dunlap, will die at the hands of Cyrus Cotton, who is also me, but not yet I. You don't know Cyrus Cotton, and I don't know him either. Yet. But we, meaning I, the writer —Murray Dunlap, a young writer with less work to his name than he would like- and you, the reader —Michael Knight, my professor, as well as the famously innovative writer whose award winning work is actually published to great acclaim- will get to know him soon enough.

I see that I've lied. I do, in fact, know Cyrus Cotton, but only intuitively. His persona is still forming as we speak, so it isn't possible to "know" him in the traditional sense. Hence, my lie. Cyrus is a character.

A Southern writer and artist who has made cameo appearances in my fiction. He has shown distaste for my work, and on occasion, remarked that the writer, his creator, me, is a gigantic fool, and, I should add, not the least bit sexy. Cyrus believes that it is disingenuous for me, the writer, to continue writing about places other than the Southeastern United States. Cyrus claims that I draw on false images when I render parts of the world other than those I have lived in. I have lived in Alabama, Tennessee, Georgia, and Virginia. I have spent a great deal of time in North and South Carolina, as well as Louisiana and Mississippi. As has Cyrus. Cyrus believes I should only write about these places, as he only writes about these places. We've both haunted the same ground.

In a recent story, I wrote Cyrus into Portland Oregon and have not reincarnated his character since. It is my suspicion that Cyrus is angry and resentful of this artistic license. I have spent only two weeks in Portland in my life. As has Cyrus. He tells me that my trees are all wrong, that my landscape is muddied with romanticized ideas about the Pacific Northwest. So I left him there. And I know he's madder than hell.

Lately I've been writing about Gray Noodle, as that is my current residence. Remember: I am Murray Dunlap, the creative writing student at the University of Theoretical Forms. I'm working on a big sexy terminal degree. You, Michael Knight, direct the program. So I've taken to stories about hiking Subconscious Canyon, road trips to Frontal Lobe, and bar hopping Repressed Points. I'm planning a trip to Split Personality, and I'll probably write about that too. All of this infuriates Cyrus, of course. He wants to live in the bowels of the humid, water-logged South. He's asked to be written into a story, a central character – no less, in which he will turn from writing to sculpture. He holds a grudge for my making him write. He claims to possess an artistic drive unachievable through the written word. Cyrus longs to sculpt. In the story, he wants to imply metaphorical balance through his construction of mobiles. He will revere Alexander Calder. Cyrus will take lessons from a beautiful black woman named Toni Morrison (who will be played by Oprah in the movie) in the abandoned welding room at the Alabama Dry Docks. He says the story will be titled "Calder's Big Sexy Fulcrum" and that it will win a big sexy contest. At least, that's what Cyrus wants.

I tell you all this only because Cyrus has recently learned some new tricks. In the story in Portland, for instance, he changed his character's home town to Jackson, Alabama. I tried to make it Knoxville as a nod to you, my innovative teacher, but somehow Cyrus jumped in between my brain and my fingers, and the letters J-a-c-k-s-o-n A-l-a-b-a-m-a appeared on the page. This very page, in fact. The one I am looking at right now. Although, you, Michael Knight, are reading these pages right now, your 'right now' and my 'right now' are off by many days.

The point is, I've become worried about the power Cyrus holds in my physical being. I am real and he is not. Correct? It is my understanding that only non-fiction characters are real, but even those are only as real as the conjured image. They are mirrors and windows. They are not the essence of the person. They do not live and breathe. But then, I, right now, am printed words on a page, which you, Michael, read as we speak. And if I am printed words on a page, then what makes me, Murray Dunlap, any more real than him, Cyrus Cotton? I see now that I have one more letter in my name. Does that help?

J-a-c-k-s-o-n A-l-a-b-a-m-a.

Perhaps not.

I can feel him in me. Moving around and tingling in my fingertips. He'll win out, of course, as I stated on the first page. No need for that sort of drama. The drama in this kind of story lies not in the 'what' of what will happen, but in the 'how.' It's a good question. How will Cyrus kill me if he is nothing more than a fiction in my head? Does he already know what he'll do? *I will kill you soon enough.* Ah, he (Cyrus Cotton) has done it (infiltrated my fingers) again. Now here, the words in italics reveal a second, competing narrator. The 'I' in that sentence is Cyrus, who is fictional, as opposed to the 'I' who is me, Murray Dunlap. And the 'you' who had previously been you, Michael Knight, is now suddenly me, the writer, the narrator, the one about to die. Shit.

I will take your gray matter into my hands and sculpt you out. Here again, the 'I' refers to Cyrus and the 'you' refers to me. Frightening, isn't it? The implied 'you' in the last sentence once again refers to you, Michael, and not me, as it had in the italicized sentence which began the paragraph.

Now, it seems that Cyrus has wiggled his way out of Portland and into the present action of my mind. I considered calling it rhyming action, but that might imply a quality of prose I can only aspire to. Clearly, this prose does not merit such a description. *My prose will not only merit the phrase, but ascend to the magical form attained by you, Michael Knight. My books will also be published and win prestigious awards.*

Holy crap. This is spectacularly interesting for two reasons. Not only has Cyrus indicated that he will function outside his role as a fictional character –he states here that he will move into the role of an *actual* writer of fiction as opposed to a character who writes fiction which doesn't exist- but he has also instigated a dialogue with you, Michael, which is distinctly separate from the dialogue we –meaning I, Murray Dunlap, and you, Michael Knight- are engaged in right now. Furthermore, look at the confident tone of his prose. It's interesting that a character within my own psyche could attain such confidence, when I, the real writer here, can barely muster the ego to type these words. Not sexy. But Cyrus, he doesn't just think he'll rub me out, he knows it.

Damn straight.

Shit.

That said, the issue of *how* he intends to kill me is still up for grabs. Will he fix me up with a pair of concrete galoshes? Will he give me a Mexican necktie? These clichéd scenarios seem impossible due to logistics. Cyrus has no physical form. He lives in my imagination. Let's "close read" his dialogue for clues: "I will take your gray matter into my hands and sculpt you out." Here, the use of "gray matter" implies a psychological killing. The clever use of the verb "sculpt" compounds the meaning. Cyrus seems to say that he, a character in my fiction, will somehow hijack my brain and maintain control of me –the writer, the very creator, the god of Cyrus- and my physical being for the remainder of my life. If so, will I, Murray Dunlap, then become a character in the prose of Cyrus Cotton? Will you, Michael, one day read a short story in *The Oxford American* wherein I, Murray Dunlap, will puppet across the page, held aloft and made to dance by the strings of Cyrus Cotton? *You will dance for me then as I have danced for you. But you will dance at a level of grace I never achieved. Richard, you will delight in the artful movements of Murray Dunlap as he becomes as real to you on the page as he once appeared in life.*

Incredible. Even as my very soul is stolen away, I can't help but marvel at the rich complexity of our situation. Cyrus has learned to interrupt my thoughts, pull my levers, and speak, with confidence, directly to you, Michael, the reader of this story. In doing this, Cyrus has already achieved his goal of becoming the actual writer. He hasn't secured permanence, but he has found a window in. Worse still, he has plans for the future. Plans that only include me, the writer, as a bit-part character in his own fiction. A character he might be inclined to punish. This does not bode well.

Bode well? What sort of a hack writer are you? These clichés are simply intolerable. Write with clarity and grace. You'd do well to learn from Michael.

Michael, you write with the hands of an artist. Murray Dunlap writes with the hands of a corpse. I'd ask you to bludgeon the fool with a pick ax if I didn't need his body. I'll admit, it's a strong body. A functional vessel. Did you know he once won the open 400 meter? Alabama State Champion. Not that he used it for anything. Never made a dime. Not even a scholarship. He turned them down to avoid the pressure. Sissy. Always running, though. Running from everything. Moves from town to town, moaning about this and that, throwing money away on therapy and booze, and all the while dragging me with him. The trip to Portland, Oregon was bad enough. Two weeks of worry over forest fires. But now this. Gray Noodle? My god this state is insufferable. It has absolutely no character of its own. But the South. Now the South has character. I will move back there soon. I will lock Murray Dunlap into a rusty dog pen behind the barn and throw rocks at him between beatings. You're welcome to come along if you like, you big sexy fiction writer.

Look at this! Cyrus maintained control for an entire thought. Two paragraphs! Well, one and a half. Nonetheless, he stayed in the moment, spoke directly to me, Murray, and you, Michael, and during the latter, managed to fling insults at my personal identity. And hit on you, Michael, but that's his business. Cyrus breeched my memories and used his own interpretation to comment on my choices in life. In the past, he's only been able to criticize my writing ability, as, of course, he lived inside the prose. But this is incredible. Cyrus now wanders my brain as if it were a library. And the hatred! My own creation, Cyrus, hates me, the writer, with the furious passion of a woman scorned. He…

Woman scorned? That's it. You're finished, Murray. I can't let another line of clichéd garbage touch the page. I've learned to stay in the moment, maintain control, and you, Murray Dunlap, I pronounce dead.

Fascinating. Cyrus has killed me. He has taken the nonmimetic concept of character and…

Seriously, you're dead.

But I'd like to comment on the literary implications of…

Nope. It's over.

But a sexy authorial commentary might…

Dead.

At last. Perfect control. I, Cyrus Cotton, Southern sculptor and sometimes writer, fictional character turned living man, own this vehicle – mind and body.

First thing, I'll move to Alabama. I'll use this tired face to convince the Dunlap family I'm in desperate need. I'll weasel my way in the door with a pitiful smile. I'll play along with old conversations. I'll laugh on cue. But soon enough, I'll take the family's house, ship them off to nursing care from an excess of 'love' in my heart. I'll raise dogs and buy a fishing boat. I'll convert the abandoned cottage into my studio. I'll write and sculpt. I'll tell the Dunlaps that Cotton is my pen name. I'll create a world of my own.

My stories will find homes in The New Yorker and The Oxford American and my sculptures will hang by thin wires from the ceilings of the MoMA and Tate. But I, Cyrus Cotton, will remain reclusive in the South. I'll encircle the property in barbed wire. I'll nail Keep Out! Signs to the dock. Mastiffs and Boxers will lumber across the lawn, growling in deep-throated rumbles. Security cameras will monitor the grounds day and night. From a windowless room, I'll eye video screens cutting from doors to gates, from the road to the water. I'll know you're coming before you know you've arrived. I'll ship out my work by paid messenger at night. My public will wonder if I am real, if I exist. They will wonder if I am Thomas Pynchon, or if Pynchon is me. They'll wonder if you, Michael Knight, penned Pynchon until bored, then invented Cotton as reprieve. I'll be investigated and scrutinized, I'll be mythologized into a god.

I am a god, of course. I created this world, did I not? I am creating even as we speak. I create a version of you, Michael, as I invent this dialogue. Your persona within these pages is a sexy invention of my own. And just as I've created you, I'll create the devil, Murray Dunlap, locked in a cage. Rise from the dead, Murray. Your peace unsettles me. I command you to awaken and feel my wrath.

I open my mouth, the nightmare cuts short, and I regain my voice. The dim light of a desk lamp pools at my hand. The cursor blinks on the computer screen in rhythm with my heart. I sit upright, lift my arms above my head and shake loose the ache from my bones. I type out a few last pages. The words materialize one by one, stretching into sentences. The lines speak to you, Michael, and attempt to speak for themselves. The writer no longer comments on the voice. The metafiction slinks into the background. The story takes on simple, straightforward prose.

Toni Morrison works out of the old welding room at the abandoned dry docks. She bought tanks of gas for the oxy-acetylene torch and scavenges scrap metal from the yard. The welding room is the size of a gymnasium. Years ago, the room would have been filled with men on task. But now, pipes, sheet metal, and trash rise up in stacks twenty feet high. A propeller the size of a Ferris wheel leans against the east wall. Toni has cleared narrow pathways through the scrap, not unlike aisles in a library. All paths lead to the center of the room. Blue light and white sparks shimmer and pulse. Toni arches over her work, practiced and meticulous, with white, black, and gunmetal gray hair pulled back in dreadlocks behind the welder's faceshield. She melts a filler rod into one side of a corner joint, forming a pool of searing liquid. With leather gloves, she presses the second half of the joint into molten steel.

Sparks bounce from her leather apron. She works the new metal into the old, mixing elements, swirling molecules into woven bonds. The joint glows red, then orange, then gray. The seam cools and hardens. The two scraps of metal have become one – perhaps an elbow or knee cap - in a fashion as natural as ice freezing between blades of grass.

Cyrus Cotton steps into the welding room and stops. He rubs his eyes, unable to see, and drops his book-bag to the ground. He smells chemicals and electrical burn. Three columns of light fall from holes in the ceiling.

No. No, I don't. This isn't the way it goes.

A clang of metal on metal reports from the center of the room, and Cyrus begins to pick his way along the path. Mice and lizards dart out of sight. Cockroaches rustle unseen. As he nears the center of the room, Cyrus pulls a twenty-dollar bill from his wallet and rolls it into the palm of his hand.

"Toni Morrison?" he asks. "Ms. Morrison?"

Don't put words in my mouth.

"Of course." Toni lifts her face mask. Her hyper-articulate voice commands attention.

"I've come for a lesson. Murray Dunlap sent me."

Please stop.

"Dunlap. All right then." She cuts off the gas to the torch. "Do you have money?"

"Twenty."

"It's twenty-five now."

Cyrus draws another bill from his wallet. He folds it against the twenty and places both on the table.

"What brings you, child?" she asks.

This is not sexy.

"I'd like to learn to sculpt."

"Be specific."

"I'd like to build a mobile," Cyrus says. "Like Calder."

I would never say that.

"Hmmm." Toni takes the welding mask off her head and sets it on the table. She removes the leather gloves.

"Do you know Calder?" he asks.

"Boy." Toni stares down the length of her father's beautiful nose. Alexander Calder, a welder himself, taught Toni the strength of a perfectly welded seam. "I know Calder."

"Sorry," he says.

Damn you! Stop putting words in my mouth.

"The question is, do *you* know Calder," she says. "And I don't want to hear a single word of what you read in some coffee table art book."

"Well." Cyrus picks at the edge of the table. The tip of his index finger turns black with soot.

"Let me put it this way. When I ask do you know Calder, what I'm really asking is do you know balance?"

"I think, I mean. Balance. Yes. Well, I know both sides of a thing need equal weight in order to balance. Or if you mean a painting, I think it means the way the components work together."

Shit. What have you done to me?

"Dear Lord." Toni dips her hand into the bib of her overalls for a gray metal sparker. "Dunlap sent you? Really?"

She puts on her gloves. She twists on the gas.

"Yes, ma'am."

"What I do here is more than sculpture. I'm trying to look at something without blinking, to see what it was like, or it could have been like, and how that had something to do with the way we live now. I step outside myself to familiarize the strange and mystify the familiar. At times, I become another person."

Toni Morrison pulls the welding mask back down over her face and squeezes the sparker with one quick motion. She ignites the torch.

"Does this interest you?"

Very, very much.

"All right then," Toni says, easing the flame against metal. "Let's get started."

Who's sexy now?

THE PHILOSOPHY OF RUNNING

IT'S MONDAY. I'M AWAKE. I'm in my shoes. I'm out the door and running.

I am a millionaire. A brand new one. I played one solitary game of poker and I won. I am a millionaire.

Like most college students, the actual 'work' of schoolwork only takes up a fraction of my time, so there's plenty of room for running. I wake up at five or six most mornings and slip on my New Balance running shoes. I've been a devoted New Balance runner since I was recruited for cross country in the sixth grade. There's a loop hole in the high school running rules that allows young runners to join the varsity team. Freshmen have to run in the freshmen division, but sixth, seventh, and eighth graders can run with varsity if they are fast enough. I was fast enough. Coach Tyson asked me to join the cross country team and I've been running ever since. And every single mile I've logged has been in New Balance shoes. They say that once a runner finds the brand that fits their foot best, to stick with it. I suppose that's why I stayed with New Balance initially, but it wasn't long before I began to appreciate the metaphorical implications of the name. I run to escape. I run to meditate. I run to breathe. Right now, for example, I am able to think clearly about myself and my family while I run. If I were sitting in a desk chair, or on someone's couch, I'd be a tangle of disjointed and fragmented thoughts. I don't say much, and I think this is why. That and the fact that my family is as screwed up as the ones you see on television. Worse, I think. At least on television they generally get a happy ending.

Everyone in the Porter family fights. All the wives and kids and one drunken father, Bennett. It's a regular American family. They nag and gossip and drink. They keep secrets and double-cross. They fight. They live in the cushion of steady allowances and the notion of a secure future based on an assumed inheritance. I guess not any more. My Daddy Bennett seemed to have arranged things to be weird and uncomfortable for us all. As usual.

Shane converted to Buddhism and has devoted his life to the river. It seems to work for him, so I'm all for it. Me, I run. Everyone else fights. I don't know what's going to happen now that I've got all the money. I can already tell they'll be acting funny toward me. Jealous, angry, spiteful. It doesn't matter, really. They all have enough to take care of themselves. No one in the Porter family is going hungry. Except at Bennett's funeral. I don't know who was in charge of that one, but they got it all wrong. This family fights, but we also eat. A day spent in all that heat cramped into that tiny church listening to that creepy fat reverend deserved a feast, one that never came. Not that it matters. Once Wallace dropped the poker bomb, no one was paying any attention anymore.

I thought I would skip the whole thing. Bow out of the game and let my hand go to someone else. I thought it would be nice if Georgia won. She should have at least gotten a hand dealt. She got a boat, but that seemed like Bennett's guilty conscience at work. But then again, she may have her own agenda and I'm not playing favorites.

I won. It's over. Another Monday, sure, but I am a millionaire.

I bought a dozen new shoes, a dozen new running shorts, and a drawer full of new socks. Three hundred dollars in top of the line, low cut socks. You can never have too many running socks. I've also come up with a plan. I'm going to run across the country. I looked it up and it turns out loads of people have done it. Some have a cause, like a dying or dead relative or spouse, and they run to raise awareness or money for whatever it was that is killing or killed the person they love.

Others do it just to do it. Like the people who hike the Appalachian Trail. Or swim the English channel. Or climb Everest or whatever. In fact, Shane says we should meet up in Wyoming and climb the Grand Teton together. Sounds fine to me. I don't know if I can do it with my limited climbing experience, but I figure by Wyoming I'll be looking for a diversion. Shane says he wants to get up into the high altitude. He said something about the Himalayas and shaving his head and getting 'above the impurity of the world.' I don't know. Climbing can be demanding and rewarding in the same way running can, so I'll give it a shot. And I always keep my head shaved. I can be out of bed and on my run without a glance in the mirror. Plus, it's hot in Massasauga. No sense in running with a wool cap on.

The thing is, I'm not sure how I'm supposed to act now that I'm a millionaire. All because the damn will forced us to play an idiotic game of cards. I knew I'd won with the first deal. Lots of discards and drawing, but it was already over. I had been dealt all the aces right off the bat. Idiotic! And yet, a fortune for me.

So I'm trying to focus on my running. And perhaps, climb to the summit of the Grand Teton and get myself purified with Shane. I need to purify. After all, the one thing I have noticed since I got the money, I need purification. And if Shane says it will, I'll try anything. Strange to come into so much for doing so little. To balance sudden wealth with an unfocused life. And run.

And so it is Monday, like any, but I need not go to a job. So, idle, I will run myself tired. And free myself from the anger itching inside of me. Monday, sure, but I am out the door and running.

RED LIGHT (A FIRE OF ITS OWN...)

Non-fiction
In memory of Frank Hardie

"The curious thing about the accident that ended my life
was that I lived through it."
Kara Swanson

BORN IN MOBILE ALABAMA, my ex-wife (from here on X) and
I are now in our mid-thirties, two careers, two dogs, no kids, and had
prepared to move back. We would again be Mobilians. Or at least, that
was the plan...

Growing up in Mobile, I lived in one house, in one bedroom,
until I was eighteen. But since finishing high school in 1992, I have
moved twenty times. I have never stayed anywhere longer than two
years. As a child, chaos is a thing oppressing you. There is no escape.
As an adult, you throw your stuff in a truck and leave. I embraced the
road. I would not be defined or confined by any community. Certainly
not Mobile. And as an aspiring writer, I thought I should be a citizen
of the world.

Our mothers still live in Mobile. That's how X and I reconnected
after six years apart. We dated in high school and then again in college
in Birmingham. We ended our roller-coaster-romance without much
ado. But six years later, when my father died, my mother told her mother
in the neighborhood grocery store. So X sent me a letter. Mobile has a
grapevine twice the speed of email. At the time, I was living in Virginia

and my ex-wife was in Oregon. One letter turned into two, which turned into emails, which turned into stomach butterflies and flights across the country.

When I started a writing program in California, X moved down from Oregon and joined me. We got married barefoot on the beach at Lake Tahoe with no one but the minister and the dog. Our mothers had mixed feelings about it, but everyone came around in the end. *How can we have a traditional wedding*, we asked? X's step-father was my father's attorney when he divorced my mother. I have two half-brothers in Seattle who I don't keep up with. I have a grandmother who is so confined by her own self-imposed schedule she did not attend my father's -her son's- funeral. *How can we possibly have a traditional wedding?* Mobile is the sort of place where everyone knows everything about everyone. Gossip is required. Imagine all the thirteen year old girls you have known. Imagine all the clicks and outcasts and the impenetrable hierarchy. Now throw that idea over an entire city like a blanket. You are imagining Mobile.

So we didn't have a wedding. But we flew to Mobile for an engagement party, for Christmas, for the various reasons that seemed to pop up every few months. When I graduated we decided to move back to the southeast, but not Mobile. Never. We wouldn't even consider it. My father had been the town drunk of sorts and X's father was (and is) a reclusive gambling addict (we assume no one knows). There was no future in Mobile. Everything in Mobile was past. My great grandfather founded a shipbuilding company there and made a fortune. But after his son was killed in the war and my father drank his life away, the fortune was gone. My father willed what was left to his fourth wife. I have a brother who lives in Birmingham with his wife and two impossibly adorable girls. They have formed their own community. They have defined themselves apart from Mobile (and good for them!). I don't know anything about my half-brothers.

X and I committed to leaving California and starting new lives in a new town. We would not be defined by a place. In an effort to be *close, but not too close*, we moved to Tennessee. The moving truck broke down twice in the desert. The rental house was a mildew circus. Jobs were not forthcoming. My book had not sold.

Then the phone rang.

X's brother had been admitted to the emergency room and was diagnosed with an extremely rare form of cancer. Everything went on hold, a constant state of panic, for two and half years. Weekend after weekend after weekend, up and down the highway. But for the last six weeks, when he had decided to stop treatment, we stayed in Mobile with him. With his wife. With X's parents. We all lived under one roof. We acted as nurses and housekeepers and medical experts and drunks and fools. We did everything we were told to do, and we guessed our way through the rest. Our friends and family, our community, had orchestrated to bring a prepared meal to our door every afternoon at 3 pm sharp. It is a powerful thing to see so many friendly faces rise together to stand by your side. Never mind the gossip and history. Like it or not, we were connected.

On Christmas day, we knew it was close. We all piled into his room for the night. At 2 am, I could hear his very slow, very shallow breathing. I shot around the room, waking everyone. We crowded the bed and told him we loved him and that everything was all right. His face, deeply jaundiced, went from pained to peaceful as he died.

So, as people do, we began to reevaluate everything. Tennessee hadn't worked out, and now we were living in Georgia. We had lost a cat and added a dog. My best friend drowned in a freak accident. My book was still unsold. Life was moving on, but not comfortably. At night, we sat on the couch and drank too much wine and talked about what the word *home* meant.

We asked ourselves, *what are we doing here?*

We dropped down to Mobile for a weekend, I forget the occasion, when I bumped into an old friend. She said the local high school, the one I attended for 13 years, was looking for a new teacher. She said I'd be perfect. She said Mobile was on the rebound. My mother-in-law was clutching X, both pairs of eyes held a look of extreme exhaustion and beautiful hope all at once, and everything I needed at the time to know (if I'd only known…) was right there in front of me.

I had looked forward to driving the moving truck down the highway. I had looked forward to taking the exit ramp down to our new, old street and parking in the shell driveway. Maybe my book would sell, maybe it wouldn't. Maybe I'd write a different book. It didn't matter. I had looked forward to spending my days teaching at the old high school and sitting up nights on the front porch with X and thinking, *here we are*. This is *where* we are. This is *who* we are.

So we moved to Mobile. We got ourselves settled into the house X's grandfather built. And we even sat on the porch and thought we would enjoy our new lives in the town we had grown up in. Had dogs in our backyard, made friends with our neighbors, anticipated my teaching job at my old high school that stood 15 minutes away. We waited patiently for our lives to begin.

And then a man ran a red-light. A man I have never met. And thus, put me in a coma for three months. Put me in a wheelchair for six months. Ended the marriage. And had me leave Mobile. I'll never teach at the old high school. I'll never live in Mobile again. It is a strange thing to have so many of life's decision's erased right in front of you. And so, I miss Frank, but I'm glad he did not have to see this. His sister and I are still friends of sorts. But it is far from the same. Very far.

And divorce was inevitable. We tried, but there was too much between us lost. Losing Frank and then my time in a wheelchair shortly after was just too much. X was overwhelmed. I see that now and I am no longer angry. I write as personal therapy. What you see right now, for example, is a way for me to sort it all out in my head. To begin to see things from a distance and not to be overwhelmed myself. X and I are still friends even. If you can imagine. Both having surmounted an impossible situation, we muddle through and admire each other's determination.

So I try to keep going. Try to keep writing. Try to stay upbeat when all I feel is down The thing is, I have much to be thankful for. I am still alive after all. I am also out of a wheelchair, no longer using a walker, and have had surgery that allows me to see without wearing a pirate patch. This Thanksgiving, I forced myself to think about this, and be thankful that I am moving on.

I move on by still writing. I am still alive and trying very hard not to go insane, so I write. My writing career actually seems to be moving along quite a bit better. To write. To breathe. To walk. To live. If Frank were here, I'd show him my book and hope that it all somehow made sense. And if it did, I'd have Frank explain it to me.

THE BURIAL OF THE DEAD

What do you feel? What do you feel?

THEY SHAVED HIS BEARD FOR THE FUNERAL. I can't begin to understand why. Who told them to do it? He looked like a pink-cheeked drag queen. But the most disturbing thing was watching my brothers squirm in that front pew. The four biggest men in this tiny church, and they shoved them all onto the front right pew. *The sons should sit together on the front row*, a man in a suit said. Who are these people making decisions? They squirmed and sweated. Massasauga, Alabama in August. If there was air conditioning, you couldn't feel it. One brother would lean forward when the other leaned back because their shoulders were too broad to sit side by side. Ren, the oldest, sat closest to the center aisle and mouthed the words *cold beer* three times through a blood red, exasperated face. I sat with the wife, ex wife, and mistress on the front left pew. The wife, Celia, sobbed and sometimes moaned into her endless cleavage. The ex-wife, Joy, had Alzheimer's and asked me four times, "Georgia, when is the movie going to start?" The mistress, Loretta – my mother, sat as rigid and lifeless as daddy. I never saw her blink. I never saw her cry. Whenever Celia moaned, mother whispered *stupid whore* to no one. As far as awkward events go, daddy's funeral was world class.

The Reverend Macallan led us in a very short, very ordinary service. He read from the bible about ashes and dust, and the organist played *Lift High the Cross*. For a moment it seemed as if it could have been a normal church service, any given Sunday.

But then the reverend wiped his brow with a white handkerchief and made more than one self-deprecating joke about his weight. Apparently there is a wine called *Fat Bastard*, and the reverend shared a bottle with Celia the night before. So much for normal.

"We got to chuckling and raised a glass to fat bastards everywhere," he said. "We found it quite appropriate, as Bennett often called me a fat bastard, and it is also how I referred to him."

"He went to Yale and I attended Harvard, so bit of good natured ribbing was only natural." The reverend winked at the congregation, which got him a few laughs, but I'm absolutely certain that at that moment, the Reverend Macallan was looking at daddy's wife.

"Stupid whore," mother whispered.

Then daddy's sister, Eleanor, walked up the center aisle with an armful of goldenrod. Eleanor is tall, thin, and stunning. She has a doctorate in psychology and a counselor's easy, welcoming face. For as long as she can remember, she has been told that she looks like Christie Brinkley. Eleanor developed a *dear me, aren't you sweet* routine that we're all sick of. She placed the goldenrod on daddy's chest, the tiny yellow flowers tickling his shaven chin. The church swished with the sounds of legs crossed and recrossed, arms crossed and uncrossed, uneasy hands rubbing, folding, and adjusting neckties. Eleanor turned and faced us and gave an audible sigh.

"As Bennett's sister, I guess I somehow knew I would be doing this someday."

Ren leaned back, which forced Baxter, the youngest, to lean forward. Baxter scratched the back of his scalp through quarter-inch hair. He adjusted his tie and coughed. He tugged the thin blonde triangle of facial hair under his bottom lip and quickly searched the room with his eyes as if mapping an escape. Despite his black suit, he wore running shoes. New Balance. Baxter never wore anything else.

"I am grateful that Bennett's struggle was short and that his pain was limited. I am happy that he was not subjected to the tortuous road so many alcoholics walk at their ends. I am relieved that Bennett died with dignity, and that he did not act out, that he did not give in to his old penchant for tantrums."

Eleanor paused, glancing up from her papers and scanning the room. I wondered if she could make out the look on our faces. Who on earth was she talking about? Not our father. Not the man who hired an acupuncturist to fly in from Seattle and heal his pain, only to laugh at the man's effeminate hands and offend him to the point of leaving unpaid. Not the man who was prescribed a painkiller that induced hallucinations and immediately mounted a disco ball over his bed and hired dancing strippers. Certainly not the man who packed a bag and moved into a hotel with the red headed Celia – one of the strippers and soon to be second wife- while his first wife, Joy, was at the hospital giving birth to Wallace, their second son. Not the man who had been dying by a slow scotch-induced-suicide for years.

Wallace sat at the far end of the pew, leaning forward and gaping at Eleanor. He had already removed his tie and used it to wipe sweat from his forehead. Then he pinched the corners of his tremendous mustache and ground his teeth. Like Ren, his face glowed red.

Between Wallace and Baxter sat Shane, the first born of the second marriage. Shane leaned back with his arms spread out across the spine of the pew. His head bobbed with sleep and then jerked back to attention. The Buddhist tattoo on his shoulder of two fish swimming in an endless circle showed through his thin white shirt. He grinned through a full red beard.

"We are all here because we loved Charles Bennett Porter, Jr." Eleanor said, reading from her papers. She stared at the typed words.

Then she looked up, took a deep breath, and chose to speak off the page.

"We loved him in our own ways. Bennett did not make it easy."

Ren looked at me across the aisle and smiled. He mouthed the words *here we go*. Celia stared, her eyes wet and starry with valium. The Reverend Macallan gripped his knees.

"Bennett was intelligent, handsome, and when we chose to be, extremely charming. But if he was charming in the last ten years, I missed it. The days of our summer sailing trips ended so very long ago. The weekends spent water skiing up on Dog River, gone. The only activity Bennett maintained to the end was hunting. He created a world of his own at the cabin in Barlo. But I believe what was once a sport for him became an outlet for anger. A very brief and very rare moment of control. He was sensitive and uncomfortable with emotion. He chose to anesthetize his feelings rather than process them. Most of his choices were self-destructive. His wives may be able to say otherwise, and I'll let them speak for themselves. The same goes for his children."

She looked at me and said, "All of them."

"I hope you have all come to terms with the ways in which you were and were not connected to Bennett. We each have to find our own way to define the relationship. We each have to find our own way to remember him, and our own way to let go."

Mother leaned in and whispered, "No one came to get their head shrunk. Bitch."

Joy leaned in and whispered, "When did Christie Brinkley start acting? She's not bad, but I sure wish they'd put more action in the plot."

"The real reason we are all here today is to mark the end of a battle," Eleanor continued. "A long difficult battle we all fought. I, for one, am glad it's over. When Bennett and I were children, when we were home from boarding schools in the summer, I loved to run outside on the very first morning and gather armfuls of goldenrod. I brought them into the house and filled vases in every room. I twisted and tied the branches and made a wreath for the front door. By the time Bennett came down from his room, his eyes had turned red with allergies and swollen to the size of soft boiled eggs. He had already sneezed a dozen times. If she was sober enough, Mom would pull the tip of his nose and say, *hello, Mr. Sneeze, let's get you medicated.*"

Eleanor walked down from the pulpit and gently patted the goldenrod lying across Bennett's chest.

"One last jab, brother," she said. "One last jab."

Then she returned to her seat.

No one else rose to speak.

We filed past daddy single file for communion. Shane placed a bowl of rice and a pint of Johnny Walker inside the casket, returning to his seat without taking any wine or bread. Celia dropped her wafer into her cleavage. Without a moment's hesitation, the Reverend Macallan plucked it out.

When we were seated again, the reverend concluded the service by proclaiming, "My peace I give to you. My peace I leave to you."

Then he led us through the side door and along a brick path to the gravesite. The brothers acted as pall bearers, lifting and guiding the pine casket easily on their shoulders. I've been told that six men would normally be required, but that after one look, the Reverend Macallan said, *four titans such as these could lift the casket if it were still inside the hearse.*

A few passages were read. Each brother dropped a handful of dirt onto the casket. Eleanor stood under the shade of a long-leaf pine and cried in silence. Celia sobbed and moaned. Mother repeated, *stupid whore, stupid whore, stupid whore.* Joy held my arm and smiled. I looked through the trees and stared at the coppery bay, perfectly still without wind. I watched a pelican glide a few feet above the surface, scanning the water for fish. I watched the pelican fly until she was out of sight, never having spotted anything worth diving for. The brothers shifted foot to foot, loosening ties and sweating. Four reddened faces with nowhere to look.

Newly shaven, our father now lay underground. Each of us brothers tried to make sense of it all, but we all scratched our heads, shrugged out shoulders, and marched out of the graveyard. There was nothing more to be done.

PAPA, I AM ABOUT TO SAIL

SOME PEOPLE SWORE THAT THE HOUSE WAS HAUNTED.

They would see lights flickering just as the river sunset.

Dog River swells with warm coppery water. The current almost imperceptible. My father, who has lived on the river his entire life, acts as if the Tigris and Euphrates met in his backyard; that all life on Earth might have begun there. Some nights he swims the river. He recites legal precedents while breast-stroking up against the current. Then, 500 yards north of the house, he'll dive 20 feet to the bottom, grab handfuls of mud and silt, and push off hard, launching his muscled body upward. At the surface, gold flashes of sunset will dance with his silhouette. He backstrokes home reciting lines of poetry. He'll time Shakespearean sonnets to his stroke. Afterward, he'll stand straight-backed at the end of the dock, closed fists on his hips, and give a passerby the illusion he has performed an act of heroism. Perhaps he apprehended a boat thief single-handed. Perhaps he rescued a drowning child from the depths of the river.

His parents built the house, both of whom are now dead. I feel certain he half expects me to move in any day. To walk barefoot down the wide hardwood planks through the long Alabama summers, to sit by him and his fire in the brief nearly forgotten winter. My nick-name, Copper, is entirely river derived. I am an only child. I will never move back home.

The property was my great grandfathers first. Mr. Clarence Sparrow. Which makes my name Copper Sparrow. Funny. Oh Alabama. So my great grandfather bought the land following the wartime shipping boom in the 40's. His once small tugboat company quadrupled in size. The cottage he built was modest, and the only extravagance he allowed himself was digging out a pond behind the house. My grandmother made an awkward plea as a child for aquatic flowers. And so, the pond was born. Mr. Sparrow was easily swayed by my grandmother. And to put the final touches on the pond, he had a tiny island of soil left in the pond's center for water lilies ... My grandmother's name was Lily. He even built an arching bridge to the island so that Lily could plant the lilies herself.

I left home at eighteen. As did everyone else. I traveled to the University of Georgia in Athens for college. I spent the minimum amount of time on my studies to keep my grades up, but far more time was spent in cafes and bars. I learned that stopping to sing "Me and Bobby McGee" with street performers both embarrassed and attracted a variety of girls. Some girls pleaded with me to stop, but others joined in. My father would not approve of any of them. In the end, I wore hippie clothing, drank red wine, smoked baggies of pot, and got on with my studies without even trying. I had inherited enough IQ that it was possible. I began attempting to grow a beard and calling my father by his first name.

"Clarence," I said. "I would like to clean up the guest cottage on the lake to stay in when I am home."

"The last hurricane ripped the duct work from the bottom," he said, "and my name is Dad or Daddy to you. Not Clarence." And with that, Clarence flicked the lights on and off repeatedly fast.

"Oh Clarence, live a little. Who cares what I call you?" I said in response to the light flickering.

"I care." Clarence shuffled his feet. "And don't you dare tell me to live a little. You need to live less, Copper."

"OK, Dad. You fix the ductwork. I'm not staying in your house, ever again."

"We'll see about that." Clarence rubbed his chin. "And keep those grades up. Stop dressing like a hippie."

So I never shaved the beard. I never moved home.

Nothing was ever the same again after that, and the haunting appeared to be of our own making ... our own squabbles, our own fugues, our desire to be better than we were. Never again would I sail.

THE RIVER

For Shane of course, and Alison, who made him whole.

THE SUCK HOLE PULLED ME OUT OF THE BOAT after spilling over pinball falls and when I got my bearings and looked up, finally knowing which way was up, I realized my foot was caught in the rocks and that, despite the short distance between my face and the surface of the roaring, rushing water, knew I was going to drown.

I can only assume that all my time spent reading about philosophy and religion is what stopped me from having a panic attack or heart attack or whatever else might happen when a person is in the act of drowning. I was calm. I bent my knees and reached down to my foot and felt the angle of the rock against my ankle. I thought I should turn my foot sideways and try kicking out of the crevice, but the water sucking against my body made it impossible to turn. My effort even seemed to tighten the pressure of the rock, and I thought about Taoist notion of doing the opposite, or doing nothing, and I relaxed. My foot stayed firmly planted in the rock, and I thought that since I was Buddhist and not Taoist, I should try something else. So I gave myself ten seconds to meditate. This may sound ridiculous, but when you are underwater and the roar and rush of a million gallons of water is sucking you down and holding you fast and you cannot reach the surface and you cannot breathe, well, in a time like that, ten seconds lasts ten hours and you will find you can meditate with profound clarity.

So in my moment of clarity, what came into focus me was that I loved my dear wife without clouds of uncertainty. None. She had taught me that to be human was to love, and that I was, in fact, whole.

A HAPPY ENDING

"HOW ARE YOU DOING, BEN?"

The camera man crunches down to take advantage of a better upshot.

"Well, I'd tell you, but there is a stranger in my house who seems to be filming us," I say with sincere astonishment.

"Pretend they're not there. None of them," my buddy says.

"And who are *they*?" I ask.

"*They* are making a movie of "us,"" he replies.

"They obvious question here, is who are "we?""

"OK pal, you asked... "We" are you and I. No faking this. And "we" are the focus of a movie that "they" are filming."

"This is seriously messed up."

"You asked," my buddy says.

"And I assume my injuries will be the focus of this 'movie'?" I ask.

"You betcha, Ben. Just maybe make your limp a bit worse for the sympathy vote."

"That is not necessary, bud. I limp, plain and simple."

"Ah, thank you," my buddy replied (for you guys at home, his name is Michael). "That sort of detail will make this movie make sense."

"And what is the point of this 'movie?'" I ask.

"It'll have people amazed to see what you have been through. How you managed to press on. To 'hang in there.' Pardon the phrase," Michael says.

"Ah, so you've seen this movie," I say.

"Yep. Watching it right now."

"My TV is busted," I say. "Watching it how?"

"We are it."

"This is a movie?"

"Yep."

"Terrible movie," I say. "Who wants to watch a guy named Michael and a guy named Ben sit around talking?"

"Well 'we' do, we're watching it right now!"

"Hmmm. Weird."

"Hey, why don't you tell us all about the wreck?"

"Cut," a distant voice calls out.

"Michael, what the hell *IS* this?" I ask sincerely.

"OK, guys." Aman who I assume is a director of some sort steps into the room. "Let's try to be more concise. And knock off on all the metanarrative crap!"

"Um, well, you are the director of some film in my living room about me. How exactly do you think I can possibly have this NOT be metanarrative?" I ask.

"Just keep going," the director says. "And talk about the wreck."

"Fine." As confused as I am right now, I'll do just that. "The wreck. Not interesting. A man none of us knows ran a red light. The end."

"And..." Michael continues, "Ben, tell us ALL what your injuries are."

"ALL?" I stammer. "This is ridiculous."

"Action!" the director calls out.

"OK, OK, Ok... I have 3 fractures in my pelvis, a broken clavicle, 9 sutures in my head, five stitches in my ear lobe, and a severe traumatic brain injury," I state.

"Brain injury!" The director calls out. "Perfect! You should riff on this... Brain injury, and traumatic too, and even SEVERE!"

"Riff? Do you want our audience, whoever they are, to think I'm nuts with a brain injury?"

"If that works..." the director stammers. "Then sure, you can be crazy!"

"I'm getting crazy mad," I reply.

"Action!" our director shouts.

"I'm really becoming angry, brain injury or not!" I shout.

"Just try again," our director says. Followed by, "Action!"

And so I made a movie, trying very hard to be 'me.' I played along, ended up on Oprah, and everyone went home happy...

"Cut!" our director shouts. "This is getting WAY too metanarrative! And give this dreadful dreariness a happy ending! Action!"

"Hmph," I start. "How to end this on a happy note? Well, the fact that a movie is being made about me is *exactly* a happy ending."

"But your audience," the director shouts. "What will they understand?"

"OK," I say. "How about a new house? You know. The cabin that I've always wanted…"

"Out of the damn budget…" our director cries. "How on earth do we pay for a house?"

"Well, you could chip in?" I stammer.

"Horseshit! Cut!" Our director looks as if he has given up.

"Hmmm," I start. "What about Oprah?"

"And why exactly, do we hope for that?" Michael says.

"Because I do care," Oprah appears from the shadows as if the whole thing was scripted out.

"Oprah… uh, uh, hello there?" I scratch my head in disbelief.

"Darling," Oprah cuts my question in half. "Anything is possible in a movie… You know that."

"So what is your part, excuse me, your *ROLE*."

"Darling," Oprah begins, "My role, as you call it, will be to help the public get a glimpse of how it is, in fact, possible to "hang in there.""

"And will this movie be it?" I ask.

"Of course, Ben," Oprah says. "And I'll give your story a happy ending!"

"How does this end?" I ask in confusion.

"Let's go see your cabin in the woods," Oprah states.

"What cabin?" I ask in utter disbelief.

"Follow me…" Oprah waves her hand to the front door and proceeds to exit my house.

"Really?" I ask as I follow Oprah onto the front porch. My question is answered when I see a shiny black limo in the drive. And of course, we then are driven to a picturesque cabin.

"Here we are, my good passengers," the limo driver says.

My goodness! I am utterly bewildered. A porch overhangs a beautiful lake. My gosh! And once the driver opens the front door, a dog comes bounding out to greet us!

"Now THIS is a happy ending!" I scream with utter amazement.

"Darling, my darling," Oprah begins, "You know that I love to give people's stories happy endings!"

"But I had no idea…" I drift into silence.

"Ahhhh, I see you like?" Oprah gives Michael and I a great big wink.

"This is awesome!" Michael interjects.

"I agree, I agree." I have to admit. "Awesome. Perfect really."

"Are you happy?" Oprah asks.

"My goodness, Oprah," I state. "Happy."

The End (credits roll for our viewers at home)

FIRES

SAWBUCK SANCTUARY BURNED to bare ashen ground in the Yacolt Fire of 1902. The fire lasted thirty-six hours. In this sliver of time, the Yacolt consumed one million acres, traveled thirty miles, and left thirty-eight dead. Nearly a century later, loose stands of immature Douglas fir, lodgepole pine, and Oregon white oak jut from a tightly meshed tinderbox of sapling and vine. Hunters poach the Sawbuck in winter, hoping to discover untapped hotspots of mule deer and bear. Instead, they return home soaked by rain and bloodied by thorns. But this is late summer. The deer drowse in tucked away corners while the landscape bakes under dry heat. Rainless thunderclouds drift in from the west, dropping fingers of ionized air across the ridge top, and with a sudden, immense surge of electricity, lightning blinks to life across the sanctuary igniting understory debris. A scatter of lost shotgun shells explodes with the crack of dynamite, and again, the Sawbuck burns.

***

THREE DAYS OUT and ten miles from her bed, Dandelion Odjick lies face up on a picnic table in Split Valley Park. This thin strip of land stretches fifteen miles. Within its borders lie open fields, two playgrounds, and a baseball diamond, all hemmed to the rocky wash of Samsara Creek. Beyond the creek, Sawbuck Sanctuary is plagued by fire. The sun drops just below the tree line on the western ridge, streaking copper shafts through white columns of smoke. Dandelion scratches at her scalp where peroxide nettled the skin. She wears three-dollar flip-flops, having traded her black leather boots for a handful of pills. Her tight black t-shirt advertises *The Sex Pistols* in red letters and the self-inflicted nose piercing swells with blood.

Dandelion lies beneath a Douglas fir, staring blankly at the branches. This fall, her mother shipped her to Portland and Webster School. They said Dandelion was *at risk*, and that Webster could *realign her spirit*. She qualified for a tuition waiver as an American Indian, but the scholarship didn't include boarding. Uncle Bud finally agreed to keep her. He forces Dandelion to share a room with his son, Garrett, who goes to Webster too. They're both in summer school. Garrett wears tie-dye t-shirts and leather sandals and hand rolls cigarettes so they'll look like joints. No one gets along.

Right now, Dandelion pretends to lie in her old backyard hammock in Alabama. The soft, twisted rope hung between two shortleaf pines. Dandelion knows those trees. She knows live oak and dogwood, longleaf and loblolly pine. Sweet gum. She knows devil's walking stick. Her father, a wannabe naturalist, labeled every tree in the yard before the divorce. Genus, species, and common name, all carefully etched into small black plates nailed to the trunk. Dandelion read the names when she snuck out to smoke stolen Camels. But here in Portland, the trees appear either foreign and nameless, or clichéd as Christmas trees. Everyone at Webster calls her Gomer. *Gaw-aw-ly*, they say. *Here comes Gomer.* Punk rock or not, her accent is impossible to miss. Dandelion watches the pinkish violet of setting sun mix with the wildfire's hot orange glow, thin rays of light splitting out between spruce needles and smoke.

"Go ahead," she says. "Burn."

Dandelion walks to the yellow plastic tunnel in the playground. Inside, she pulls a can of Ravioli from a paper bag. On hands and knees she digs a pocketknife from her hip pocket and clicks open the hook shaped blade. She works her way around the lip, carefully shifting the can an inch at a time with her left hand while her right works the knife. Opened, the can looks small. A few bites and it's gone.

The smell of smoke is strong now and she climbs out of the tunnel to scan the tree line. The sun has dipped beneath the mountain, but the metallic orange sky, if anything, glows brighter. Still hungry, she crushes her last pill on a metal swing seat and snorts it through the hollow tube of a ballpoint pen. Ritalin takes the edge off her hunger. She pitches the tube into the branches of the Douglas fir. She wants to stay close to the fire, her eyes falling into hypnotic glaze, but the smoke is getting thick and she turns away in fear. Dandelion makes her way across the outfield and begins to climb the wooded eastern slope.

***

ELOISE SPINNAKER PARKS HER BLACK MERCEDES in the drive at four-thirty, stubbing out a cigarette and exhaling one shallow wisp of smoke. The house clings to a steep hillside, an assembly of sharp modern angles on stilts four stories high, perfectly maintained, blanched in sunlight. Stepping out of the coupe, Eloise pushes the leather seat forward and retrieves three boxes of sushi hors d'oeuvres from the back. She carries the boxes into the kitchen where she places them on a marble counter along with her purse and keys. She clears a space in the refrigerator and slides in the sushi. Eloise returns to the car and hefts out a new green garden hose. She already owns a yellow spray nozzle, adjustable to ten different settings. Stream/pulse is her favorite.

Eloise carries the hose to the patio beside the pool, then returns to the car for a small white bag in the passenger seat. She carries the bag into her bathroom. She sits at the second vanity. Inside the bag, she retrieves three pill bottles and places them on the counter. Nembutal, Valium, and Dexedrin. Eloise fills a glass with Evian and swallows two Dexedrin. In the top left drawer of her vanity, Eloise removes a small blue and white Chinese sugar service and a syringe. She sifts auburn hair through her fingers, taps out five Nembutal, and crushes them with a spoon. She empties the spoon into the sugar bowl, drizzles in Evian water, and stirs the two together. Submerging the needle, she draws the solution into the translucent cylinder. With her thumb, she gently prods the plunger until the first drop of liquid swells into a bead at the needle's tip. She lifts her leg and props her foot against the edge of the counter. Eloise sinks the needle between her toes.

Hayden Spinnaker pulls into the garage at six. The glove box sits open and he reaches over for his flask. Torn white envelopes of bank statements and mortgage papers and an overfull manila folder clutter the passenger seat. The portfolio within the folder details quarterly losses. Dog-eared pages with highlighted passages have been crumpled, then smoothed again. The radio burbles out the location, size, and intensity of forest fires burning up and down the Oregon coastline. They've named the expanse of fires *Vulcan's Hearth*. Fire Commander Cyrus Cotton reports from the field:

> *Air tankers dropped fire retardant in strategic locations, but in some areas heavy smoke and dangerous wind conditions made airdrops impossible. Crews from Tillamook, Glenwood, Gales Creek, Newberg, and Forest Grove are working around the clock. Residents of surrounding areas should prepare for evacuations. They are voluntary right now, but I expect mandatory evacuations within the next 48 hours. It may become necessary to light backfires in order to stop the blaze.*

Hayden takes a pull from his flask. Pressing a luminous red button, Commander Cotton is instantly replaced with Charlie Mingus. "Party tonight," Hayden says aloud. The vodka warms his throat. Hayden presses a console switch and the driver's side window groans down an inch. A .38 revolver lies hidden under his seat. He rests his forehead on the leather wrapped steering wheel, thin blonde hair mopping the dash, and cradles the flask in his crotch. A pack of cigarettes sits wedged under the emergency brake. He lifts the brake and retrieves the pack. Hayden listens to Mingus fingering strings on *Mood Indigo*. He lights a cigarette, draws smoke. He holds it in his lungs.

Beside the house and beyond the eight by twelve wading pool, Eloise stands barefoot in a puddle of water. She holds the yellow spray nozzle in her left hand and tugs on the hose with her right. Choppy bursts of water launch into tree limbs, eye level from the concrete deck. The cost of building the pool onto the side of the mountain peaked out at over seventy-five thousand dollars, but Hayden insisted that a house is incomplete without one. Just this morning, Eloise submerged herself naked beneath the heated water. She peered over the lip of the pool, her lithe, pale legs fluttering out behind her, and watched children play baseball in the park below. From this height, the children were only specks of movement tittering about the orange dirt. Eloise rested her chin on a forearm, her breasts pressing against cool ceramic tiles, and recited the Tibetan phrase, *namas-te*, over and over again. Her lips barely parted as she spoke.

Hayden steps out of the house through sliding glass and squints in the summer sun. Beads of water wink off hemlock needles bright as Christmas lights.

"What are you doing?" Hayden asks.

Eloise takes three sideways steps and continues to spray the trees.

"That won't help," he says.

"There's a case of wine in the trunk of my car. Do you think you could take it into the kitchen?" she asks.

"Your trunk. In this heat." Hayden cups his hand over his eyes. "It's ruined."

"The Singletons left a message saying they'll be a bit late. I imagine the Archers will be late as well. They're always late."

"I need to shower," he says. "Did you get the ring from the vault?"

Eloise glances back through dilated pupils. "The wine first, Hayden. It's not ruined."

"What we really need is for the wind to stop." Hayden hops over the hose as Eloise pulls it around the pool. "Or blow the other way."

"The wine, Hayden. Our guests will want wine when they get here. No one is going to evacuate." Eloise releases the trigger on the nozzle and the water stops. "I think I'll float candles in the pool. Won't that be lovely?"

"Did you get the ring from the vault?"

"Yes, Hayden."

"Riley will want to see the ring."

"The wine, Hayden."

***

THE SINGLETONS ARRIVE AT EIGHT-FIFTEEN, the Archers at eight forty-five. A Haitian housekeeper offers plates of sushi and glasses of Pinot Gris. At Eloise's request, she serves the guests in a kimono and silk slippers. Riley Singleton, a once-renowned lapidary for De Beers, passes on wine and carries a short glass of scotch. Hayden met Riley when he inquired into imposing an impossibly delicate cut on an 8-carat family diamond. The stone had been his grandmother's, a colorless pear cut, and slightly shallow in terms of light dispersal. Hayden flew to Tel Aviv and asked Riley to transform this imperfect stone into a flawless, round cut. The trick of it lay in Hayden's demand that the weight remain above seven carats. Riley warned Hayden that re-cutting this thinly might create flaws, microscopic fissures. But after viewing the stone with a Firescope, Riley dismissed his own fears and took the challenge. He valued the finished product at seven hundred and fifty thousand dollars and delivered it personally to Hayden's hotel suite. The Portland Chronicle devoted a thousand words to the story. Now, five years later, Riley lives in Portland as well. He works in appraisals, having retired from cutting. As for the diamond, it sits on Eloise's ring finger, ticking against her glass and scintillating the pale gold of her wine.

Ian Archer peers through the drapes, cupping his hands against reflecting light. "The fire is close," he says.

"Please, please. Let's not open the drapes," Eloise says. She begins whispering under her breath, eyes to the ceiling.

"Hayden, the tree line on the next ridge is glowing," Ian says. He shifts his weight off of his prosthetic leg.

"I'll turn on the news," Hayden says. He reaches for the remote control.

"No, No. Not now please," Eloise says. "Please, let's not turn on the TV. Be a dear and close those drapes, Ian."

Riley rubs his left index finger across his right index finger, pointing at Ian. "You've upset the queen. Better straighten up."

"The park," Hayden says. "I say we wait to see if the fire makes it to the park. If it makes it that far, we should evacuate. Keep the drapes open."

"An evacuation!" Riley shouts in throaty baritone. "Let's drink to the evacuation."

"I'll have another glass of wine," Chelsea Archer says.

"As will I," adds Tiffany Singleton. She lifts her empty glass and rocks it side to side. Her skin is flawless, her eyes a shimmer of green.

"Wonderful," Eloise says. She nods to Hayden. "Do bring in another bottle please."

"Riley, help me in the kitchen," Hayden says.

"Sir, yes sir!" Riley snaps a stiff hand to his wide forehead and draws his heels together in one awkward movement. "I could use a fresh glass myself."

"Dearest Chelsea," Eloise says, cocking her left brow. "Could you help me for a moment up in my room?"

"Why of course my dear," Chelsea says.

All four exit, leaving Ian and Tiffany in the sitting room. Ian sips wine. Tiffany checks her face in a silver-plated compact. She wiggles her strapless dress into place before stepping to the window.

"Should we worry? The lady on the news said fires could spread very quickly."

"They use a formula to predict it. Wind speed, vegetation height, and moisture content." Ian puts down the glass and animates his words with hand gestures. "If a fire gets hot at the base of a mountain, and if it's bone dry, it can climb the incline at ninety miles an hour."

Tiffany presses cupped hands to the glass and peers out at the tree line. An undulating pale yellow clings to the crowns of spruce and fir. The sky beyond the trees has oxidized to rust. She glances down at the steep slope beneath her.

"Oh dear. We should worry. Should we worry?"

"I'm giving it one hour." Ian says, holding up a finger. "If that glow gets any brighter or any closer in an hour, I'm leaving."

"Oh dear," Tiffany says. She excuses herself to the restroom.

***

DANDELION'S HANDS, blackened with soil and sweat, begin to shake. Her breath turns as brittle and labored as that of an old woman. Digging in with her fingers, she angles her feet sideways and pushes herself up the steep incline one step at a time. The air begins to clear as she climbs, but her eyes still burn with smoke from the valley. Above her, Dandelion can just make out the halos of streetlights; house windows alight in soft yellow. The houses float among the trees. They appear as tall and thin as church spires. She props her feet on the base of a Sitka spruce and lies back against the hillside. As if trespassed upon, a neighborhood dog begins to bark in earnest.

A banana slug sits on a browning leaf next to her hand. The slug, five inches long and thick as a Cuban cigar, explores the air with two sets of telescoping antennae. As she watches, the antennae retract for reasons unseen. Last week, Garrett told Dandelion about them. He explained that banana slugs eat mushrooms and then secrete special oils, toxic to birds and snakes. *But Gomer,* Garrett said, *they'll get you really high.* Garrett pinched the base of a black marker with his right hand and wiggled it as if it were alive. He slid his fingernail down the back of the pretend slug with his left hand, and then spread the imagined slime onto a scrap of paper from his notebook. The teacher faced the blackboard and wrote *hear ye! The godless are dull and the dull are damned.* Garrett rolled the paper, brought it to his lips, and with closed eyes, inhaled deeply. He held it. Exhaling, Garrett howled with laughter. Dandelion called him *a disgusting fuck.* The teacher turned and called them both to the front, handing each a sheet of paper. *Read,* he said. Garrett stammered over his words, reciting: *at dusk, just when, the light is filled with birds, seriously, I begin…* The bell cut him short. Dandelion hooked her backpack with one hand and made for the door. The teacher stopped her mid-room. *Your turn will come Monday, Miss Odjick.*

Dandelion did not attend class on Monday. Or Tuesday. And now, wrapped in gauzy darkness on a steep hillside with Wednesday spooled out behind her, she wonders if she'll go back at all. Dandelion picks up the slug and holds it beneath her nose. The slug is odorless.

"We don't have your kind in Alabama," she says. "You're ugly."

She drags a fingernail across its glistening yellow back, smells her finger. Nothing. She lightly touches fingertip to tongue. Nothing there either. So she licks the slime from her nail. At once, she hypersalivates as if biting into a salted lemon slice. She dry-heaves. Her mouth seems to go numb. Dandelion holds the base of the spruce tree, spitting, tears falling into the powder dry soil. "You hippie bastard," she cries out. "You-lying-son-of-a-bitch-pervert-hippie-bastard!"

Dandelion continues climbing the hill, cussing Garrett. She hacks and spits, her tongue a wad of putty. The incline eases to a manageable grade and Dandelion is able to stand. She steps up between a crosshatch of hemlock limbs and finds herself at the base of a house, a towering structure with multiple balconies, soft lights flickering above a deck on the second level. Basement windows reflect darkness divided by a pale strip of orange, wavering at the horizon. Dandelion turns to the wildfire. Smoke crawls through new moonlight, sprawling the length of the sky. The bottom fringe of cloud blushes crimson. Above it, patches of white intermittently burst with color. Dandelion stares. She can't decide if she is excited or afraid.

***

IN THE BEDROOM, Eloise pulls Chelsea in and shuts the door.

"How's Ian?" Eloise asks. "He seems so, I don't know, uptight."

"He's fine." Chelsea speaks in singsong tones. "We're fine. Everyone's fine." Chelsea turns to the bedroom's small gas fireplace. An antique Japanese screen conceals the false logs. The screen depicts an Okame figure, finely rendered, on two silk-screened panels. Okame stands coyly in a pale green kimono, forearms raised and hands cocked forward at the wrist while she leers down upon a mushroom dangling in a snare. The mushroom hangs by a string tied around its thick shaft, the rounded cap pointing toward Okame. A wolf hides behind a bale of hay, hoping Okame will take the bait. In his paws, the wolf holds a lariat.

"How's therapy?" Chelsea asks.

"Namas-te," Eloise chants.

Chelsea looks over her shoulder, furrows her brow.

"My new mantra."

"What's it mean?"

"I salute the spirit within you."

"I thought that was Star Wars."

"No, that's *the force*. This is from Tibet." Eloise takes a deep breath. "Naaa maas teee. It's both a greeting and farewell. Like *aloha*."

"Does it help?"

"It's calming. And it sounds exotic. I think that's what I like about it." Eloise drums her fingers on a Beijing coffer, hand carved from oiled camphor. "How's Ian getting on with the new company?"

"Ian says they'll have to liquidate assets." Chelsea pulls at her skirt, smoothing over the surface of textured linen. She pats the underside of her brassy shoulder length curls. "He's not sure he can bail them out. He thinks it's going to be a very hard recovery."

Eloise sits on the bed and rubs her flattened palm in a circle on the duvet. "How is everything else?"

"Very hard," Chelsea smirks. Then she sits next to Eloise. "I don't know, I think he still worries about the leg. It doesn't bother me, it never has. But I think he thinks it does. And then there's the guilt. The prosthetic reminds him of the wreck. And the slut. That poor dead slut. He'll carry that with him for life."

"We've all made mistakes," Eloise says. "All of us."

"You're right," Chelsea says. She stares at the Japanese screen. "How far up does the prosthetic go?"

"Almost all the way. He's got a bit of thigh. Maybe three or four inches."

"I hope the surgeon left a few more inches next door." Eloise raises her eyebrows.

"And then some," Chelsea says.

Both women laugh, stopping abruptly at some distant sound, unregistered and out of place.

"What was that?"

"Who cares," Eloise says. "Let Hayden handle it."

"And how *is* Hayden?"

"Cold, distant." Eloise pauses. "If he's hard, I don't know about it."

"And you?"

"Therapy, Tibetan chants, and our little friends." Eloise motions into the bathroom, heels clicking onto ornate, hand-painted tiles. Tiny Geishas gaze up from the floor.

"I'm running low," Eloise says.

"Already?"

"You can get more, right?"

"The other nurses are suspicious." Chelsea slants her eyes, looks left, then right.

"You said they're all addicts."

"I said some of them are. Not all."

Eloise slides a pill from a bottle with her finger. "I got a little using my prescription at the pharmacy, but it won't last."

"I know."

"So." Eloise swallows the pill with her wine.

"Do you have the money?"

"Yes."

"All of it?"

"Yes."

"Ok then," Chelsea says. "You know it's going to kill us, my dear."

"Ah, yes," Eloise giggles. "Dead as hammers, I suppose."

***

CYRUS COTTON KNOWS SAWBUCK SANCTUARY. Under the safety of rain, he hikes the trails through winter. He knows of an isolated cave, hidden within the steep mountains. Inside, he's built a makeshift cot and hooked a lantern to the ceiling. If he finds poached game, he'll skin it out and keep the hide. His cot is warm. He will spend two weeks vacation in this backcountry alone. He knows every dip and curve of Samsara Creek. He knows the deer paths and where they rut. He knows the bears by their markings and gives names to the cubs. Cotton holds the topography of the Sawbuck in his mind as easily as his mother's face.

***

TIFFANY FINDS THE SPINNAKER guest bathroom glossed in dim light. She turns on the vanity and ceiling lamp. She studies herself in the mirror. Tiffany pulls a mascara wand from her purse and gently curls her lashes. She pencils in fresh eyeliner. Applies powder. Plucks from her brow. She steps out of her dress and checks the tape beneath her breasts. With skilled hands, she adds a new strip to enhance the lift. For the final examination, Tiffany leans into the countertop and checks her work. She loses herself in the mirror, searching every follicle, every pore. She leans so close, her nose nearly touches the reflection. Her calves tremble, unnoticed. She wishes the face-lift could pull more tightly. She wishes her eyes were really green. She wishes her implants were filled with helium so they might float like balloons.

***

DANDELION PULLS OPEN an unlocked basement door. She steps in carefully, hoping for water, a sink, something to rinse her mouth, but the basement dissembles in darkness. She extends her arms, hands palm out, and slides her feet forward on the rug. Mid-room, her toes bump against steel. She gropes cold metal bars, rubber grips. Her hand skims the surface of the metal, finding a bicycle seat. She continues to search, feeling her way down the length of a couch. Beyond that, an end table and lamp. Dandelion reaches under the lampshade. She fingers the knob, not sure whether to push, pull, or twist. The bulb clicks on just in time to highlight the lamp's descent to the floor. For a moment, Dandelion sees a blue and white vase and rice paper shade. The vase cracks open and the rice paper tears, all followed by a pop and flash of white light. Then darkness.

Dandelion turns, but cannot see her way out. She fumbles blind into a wall and slides quaking hands along the surface. She bumps into a chair, table, and floor lamp. Discovering a new door, she reaches inside, frantic for light. Finally, a row of incandescent bulbs ignites above a mirror. Dandelion quickly scans the bathroom and looks back to the basement. Couch, stationary bicycle, and then it's ten yards to the outside door. She hears voices upstairs. Her tongue burns. In an instant, Dandelion hides in the bathroom, cuts the lights, and crams her head under a bathroom faucet. She cups water onto her extended, lapping tongue.

***

IN THE KITCHEN, Riley drains a scotch, neat, and pours another. Hayden gulps a fresh vodka and pours four glasses of wine. A crash from somewhere in the house echoes into the room.

"Hell was that?" Riley asks.

"Got me."

"How are things in Hayden-land these days?" Riley squeezes Hayden's shoulder with strong hands. "Still selling short, trading on margins? What are you into now?"

"I'm trying to write a real time program that will auto sell on pre-set quotes. It'll work like Datek, but better. I need to free up some time to keep an eye on the volatile ones. Recently, I've taken some losses." Hayden takes a step back, Riley's hand slipping off. Riley makes a fist, then pats the countertop.

"*Dogs of the Dow* for me," Riley says. "Been at sixteen percent since '63."

"I think that's about how my portfolio looked in '63."

"You were ten years old in 1963."

"I was already invested."

"Silver spooned motherfucker." Riley grins. "I learned a skill. Worked for a living." He arches his back and sets his jaw. He pounds his chest with closed fists. Both men laugh.

"I wanted more than sixteen percent," Hayden says.

"Where are you now?"

"Hard to say." Hayden looks up from the floor, crosses his arms. "If the house burns down, I'll build another one."

"Now that's a big man talking there." Riley pauses. "Wait, they won't insure this place?"

"No. They say the property is an *extreme risk zone*. But we have Eloise's ring."

"An insurance policy in and of itself."

"You got it." Hayden pours another scotch for Riley. "Speaking of, I need a new appraisal. If you don't mind, of course. For insurance."

"You don't need that." Riley says. "It hasn't been very long. Keep your figures."

"I'd still like one," Hayden says. "For insurance."

Under hot kitchen lights, the cut crystal glass sparks flashes of gold as Riley pivots his wrist. "It's just a goddamned stone, Hayden. A pebble." Riley looks down, unbuttons his jacket. He shuts his eyes in deep concentration.

"What the hell's the matter with you?" Hayden presses both hands against Riley's chest. "It's a motherfucking diamond."

***

"EVERYTHING OK?" Ian asks.

"Of course," Tiffany says. "Why?"

"You've been gone a while."

"Girls will be girls."

"Yes, I suppose." Ian resists the urge to reach down to his leg. He knows that the pain, as well as the leg, exists only in his mind.

"I think Chelsea is on something," Ian says.

"I think you might be right," Tiffany says.

Ian snaps his head left. "What do you know?"

"Nothing. Just that she's not the friend she used to be."

"But do you know what's she's taking?"

"She's a nurse, Ian. She can take whatever she wants."

A sound like breaking glass rises from the stairwell. Ian and Tiffany stop talking and turn from the window, faces gone slack.

"My God," Tiffany says. "First wildfires, now we're tearing things apart. What a splendid evening."

"Is anyone downstairs?" Ian asks.

"I don't believe so," Tiffany says. "The ladies are gossiping in the bedroom and the men are in the kitchen getting drunk. Eloise sent the housekeeper home."

"Well that noise came from downstairs."

"At least, I think she sent the housekeeper home." Tiffany curls glossy black hair behind her ear.

"Housekeeper or not, someone is down there."

"My God."

Ian and Tiffany lean over the banister and search the darkness.

"So what's the fuss about?" Eloise asks.

Ian and Tiffany, still leaning against the banister, look up as Eloise and Chelsea enter the room. In the same moment, Riley and Hayden reappear from the kitchen. Hayden holds a tray of drinks, rocking enough to slosh wine as he walks. Riley dips his finger into scotch and lightly rubs the rim of his glass. The crystal sings with vibration.

"Cut it out, Riley," Ian says. "We think there's someone downstairs."

Hayden sets down the tray. "What, like a burglar?"

"Is the housekeeper still here?" Tiffany asks.

"She shouldn't be," Eloise says. "But she must. Who else could it be? It must be the housekeeper."

"Or no one," Riley says. "Have you looked? We don't know that there's anyone down there."

Chelsea lifts one of the wine glasses from the tray. "Very true," she says. She shrugs very small shoulders and gulps the wine.

Riley walks to the banister and squeezes between Ian and Tiffany. "Hello down there," he shouts. "Anyone home?"

Silence.

"Dammit Riley," Ian says. "Now they know we know. We should call the police." Ian feels a tingle where his leg used to be. He scratches aluminum beneath his pants.

"Heaven's sake." Eloise arches her eyebrows. "No one is calling the police. Hayden, go look in the basement."

"Me too," Riley says. "Let's flush 'em out."

"We really did hear something," Ian says, still scratching. "I'm not making this up."

Riley takes three steps down the stairs, stops, and raises his chin, "Ian, you're a pansy." He resumes his descent to the basement.

Riley sees the broken lamp first thing. He sips his drink and hovers over shards of vase. He splits an ice cube with his teeth, grinds it to nothing. Mud tracks dot the rug.

"Anything?"

"Yep." Riley turns to Hayden at the base of the stairs. "Somebody's been in here."

"I'll call the cops," Hayden says.

"It doesn't look like they took anything. Just a busted lamp. I'd forget it."

"Forget it?" Hayden takes another step into the room. "Are you kidding me?"

"Cops will be a hassle," Riley says. "I'd forget it. Let it go. It's probably a homeless guy. No harm done."

"No harm done?" Hayden stares at Riley five full seconds. "How do we know they've gone?"

"Only other place is the bathroom." Riley finishes his drink. "Why would they hide in the bathroom when the door is right there?"

"What if it's a psycho killer? Has it occurred to you that the intruder might not be exactly right in the head?"

"Say, does anyone ride this thing?" Riley grabs the bike handles and feigns physical exertion.

"Someone could be in there right now."

"Only one way to find out." Riley balances his glass on the bicycle seat and turns to the bathroom. He extends his right hand, palm out, when the door jerks open.

***

VULCAN'S HEARTH BURNS to the heart of the Sawbuck. Cotton's cave, once covered by thorny brush, now lies exposed. A sloth of bears gathers in the rear of the cave and cowers from heat and smoke. Cotton knows this. And he knows they will not all survive. He collects his men and explains a new plan. *Backfire,* he says. *That's how we stop it.* He lectures them on tactics and safety. He pops a stick against a giant map. *Here, here, and here,* he says. The men watch and listen. They crack knuckles and tap feet. They double-knot their boots. When Cotton stops speaking, they stand and nod before stepping out into night.

***

"JESUS CHRIST!" Riley shouts.

Dandelion bolts through the door, juking Riley with a spin. Her right flip-flop pops off, shooting backward against the wall. Her left ankle turns. A surge of pain fires up her leg. She makes a quick stride and hurdles the exercise bike. The first leg clears the center bar but her trailing knee strikes it dead center, sending Dandelion to the floor. Riley's glass falls with her, cracking apart against a thin rug on a hard floor. Crystal fragments ring the girl's head.

"It's a damn kid." Riley says.

Hayden stands immobile. Lips parted, breathless.

Dandelion lies on the floor, eyes pinched shut, and clenches her ankle with both hands. "I didn't steal anything," she says. "I didn't steal anything!"

Tiffany, Ian, Chelsea, and Eloise crouch at the top of the stairs, peering between banister spindles. Ian leans at an awkward angle, unable to fully flex his artificial knee. Tiffany fingers her hair.

"Calm down," Riley says.

"I didn't steal *anything.*"

"Ok, we got it." Riley squats beside Dandelion. "What's your name, sweetheart?"

"Dandelion Odjick."

"All right, Dandelion Odjick. You live around here?"

"A few miles off, I guess."

"You have a daddy I can call."

"No." Dandelion stares at Riley.

"A mother?" Riley asks.

"Three thousand miles away."

"All right, Dandelion. What say we get you upstairs and have a look at that ankle."

In the sitting room, Dandelion slouches in a leather chair with both legs propped up on the ottoman. Chelsea cradles the heel of her foot in her palm.

"Does this hurt?" she asks, applying gentle pressure to one side.

"God, yes," she says.

"How about this?" Chelsea turns her foot in the opposite direction.

"Oh my fucking God!" Dandelion heaves upright. Her hands grip and crease the once smooth leather.

"There's a mouth on that one," Tiffany says.

"And an accent," Riley says. "Where are you from?"

"Alabama."

"Sprained ankle it is," Chelsea says. "But have it X-rayed to be sure."

Hayden stands with arms crossed. He nods his head at the floor, begins to pace. He rolls up powder blue shirtsleeves and crosses his arms again. Eloise sits on the couch, head lolling backward, eyes closed. She whispers *namas-te* as if no one can hear. Tiffany and Riley crowd behind Chelsea, watching her watch Dandelion. Ian has moved to the other side of the room and watches a blonde reporter interview Cotton. Cotton watches the fire from the corner of his eye.

Hayden suddenly stops pacing, "What were you after?"

"I told you I didn't take anything," Dandelion says.

"But what were you after? Why did you come here?" Hayden says.

"Come on Hayden," Riley says. He looks at Dandelion. "You're what, fourteen?"

"Fifteen," Dandelion says. "Look, all I wanted was to get away from the fire. We didn't have fires like this in Alabama. The only ones I ever saw were set on purpose."

"They say lightning started this fire," Ian says.

"Hell, I forgot all about it," Riley says. "What are they saying, Ian?"

Ian laces his fingers together and continues to watch the blonde reporter.

"Not speaking to me, huh." Riley stands and walks to the television. He turns up the volume. Everyone watches in silence except Hayden, who paces the floor. Cotton explains his plan.

"My word," Chelsea says. "They're going to light a backfire from Split Valley Park?"

"That's at the bottom of the hill," Eloise says. "Isn't one fire enough?"

"You would think," Chelsea says.

"I also came in to get some water," Dandelion says.

"My God," Tiffany says. "I'll get some for the poor girl." She pads to the kitchen shoeless, pantyhose swishing on hardwood.

"Where do you live?" Chelsea asks.

"With my uncle," Dandelion says. "He's a drunk."

"You're Native American, aren't you?" Eloise asks.

"Half, unless money is involved. Then I'm full Algonquin."

"You see," Ian pulls his hands apart and begins to gesture in the air. "They light a backfire when the wind conditions are favorable. For us, that means the wind must have turned. Must be coming in from the east." Ian thumbs the air in an easterly direction. "The idea is to burn a stretch of land before the wildfire gets there. That way, the wildfire has nowhere to go. If they light a backfire in the park, it'll burn away from us. It'll climb that ridge on the west side of the valley and keep the fire from ever reaching our side. It's all preserved land over there. I think they call it the Sawbuck. No houses at all, just trees."

"What if the wind shifts and blows the fire right back at us?" Hayden asks.

"Then you're screwed," Riley says. He places his glass on the coffee table. "But like you said, Hayden. You'll just build another house."

"Could you teach us a chant? Or a tribal dance?" Eloise asks.

"You're slurring, dear," Tiffany says, returning with the water. She hands the glass to Dandelion. When Tiffany leans in, she peers at her breasts.

"What were you after?" Hayden asks Dandelion. He stands over the chair. "Did you come for the diamond?"

"She's a kid," Riley says. "What's she know about diamonds?"

"I just wanted some water," Dandelion says. She sinks deeper into the chair.

"You came for the diamond. Everyone knows about it."

Eloise begins a jerky march around the couch, popping her outstretched fingers against her mouth and humming.

"What diamond?" Dandelion shouts. "I don't know what you're talking about." Dandelion tries to get up. She winces and drops back into the chair.

"Dammit, Hayden. Let it go." Riley gets to his feet. He sways with booze.

"Have another drink, Riley."

"I'm trying to tell you something here."

Hayden turns again to Dandelion. "I could have you arrested for breaking and entering."

"Hayden," Chelsea says.

"I'm trying to tell you something, Hayden." Riley palms sweat from his forehead.

Eloise forgets why she's dancing and sits back on the couch.

"Tell me you knew about the diamond," Hayden says. "Admit it."

"She's just a little girl," Tiffany says, then turns her head. "Sit down Riley. You're drunk."

"Admit it!" Hayden shouts. "You-"

"The diamond is flawed," Riley says. He stands motionless.

"What?" Hayden asks.

"The cut was too thin." Riley takes a deep breath, releases. "Now there's a fissure, a crack, running the edge of the stone." He glances around the room. All eyes are on him except for Eloise. She holds the ring an inch from her eye.

"You can't see it." Riley says. "It's microscopic."

On the television, a mud-flecked truck rumbles toward the park. An unlit flamethrower mounted to the flatbed points skyward. Men in yellow jackets with oversized helmets crouch next to the flamethrower. Their eyes shine with confidence.

Hayden shoves his hands into his pockets and marches into the kitchen. From the sitting room, they hear ice cubes dropping into a glass. When the vodka is poured, the ice cracks and pops.

"You can see the park from the deck," Chelsea says. "Let's have a look."

Riley steps over to Dandelion, lowers his shoulder. "Come on, I'll help you walk."

She recoils from his touch, instantly pushing herself into the side of the chair. Riley pulls his hand back. Then he exhales and his eyes go soft. When he tries again, she lets him lift her. She holds him tight.

***

LIT CANDLES FLOAT IN THE POOL, reflected in flickers on tree limbs hanging from above. Through the trees, they peer down into the valley. Wildly bright bursts of flame shoot out into the far ridge, igniting trees and billowing smoke. Ashes and embers swirl like fireflies while flames whip and curl, jumping quickly to the top of Sawbuck ridge. It is too far and too dark to make out individual people, but they know Cotton is there just the same. He coordinates the men, the flame-thrower, the axes and shovels. They watch the fires, both wild and controlled, illuminating the contours of oversized trucks crawling across the fields. Samsara Creek has grown so hot that fish rise to the surface, white bellies slipping away downstream.

Dandelion stands on one leg, her left arm over Riley's shoulder. Riley's right arm grips her side. Ian stands next to them, gesturing wordlessly with his hands, absorbed by the view.

"Hey," Dandelion says, pointing to the nearest tree. "That's hemlock."

"Western hemlock," Ian says. "*Tsuga heterophylla.*"

"I know Eastern hemlock, *Tsuga anadensis.*" Dandelion smiles, takes an extended branch into her right hand and smells it. "Same needles, flat and rounded. Same color green." Reminded of home, the smile disappears. She'd give anything to be there now. Looking up, white smoke etches the pendulous treetop into perfect silhouette.

"That highest branch," Dandelion says. "It bends over the exact same way."

"You call that the leader," Ian says.

"I knew that," Dandelion says. "When I move back to Alabama, I'll send you a picture of anadensis."

Through the den window, Tiffany watches Cotton on television without sound. Soot smears the faces of firemen passing behind Cotton, but his remains clean. He speaks with animation, arching his eyebrows and curling his lips. He lifts his hands for emphasis. She wonders how old he might be, and how he cares for his skin.

"Did you know that without fire, giant sequoia trees are unable to reproduce?" Ian says. "The seeds need bare soil to germinate. That's only possible after a fire has cleared away debris from the ground." Ian spreads his arms and unfurls his fingers as if completing a magic trick. "As we speak, the youngest sequoia trees are already over a century old."

"Well, it looks like these trees won't have to burn."

Riley watches the backfire, then turns to the house. "You're right, Dandelion. I think we've been spared."

A muffled pop sounds from inside the house. For now, it goes unnoticed.

Tiffany, Chelsea, and Eloise huddle together. They've turned to sit against the edge of the deck wall with their backs to the fire. Eloise holds her hand out as if reaching for the pool. The wind picks up from the west. She turns her hand side to side, catching glints of blue light against the diamond.

"Well, it's beautiful just the same," Chelsea says. "Even if it isn't valuable."

"Yes," Tiffany says. "It *is* very beautiful."

"You know," Eloise says. "It may be the only beautiful thing here."

"What's that supposed to mean?" Tiffany asks.

Eloise lifts her head and clasps both hands against her chest. She shuts her eyes.

"It doesn't mean anything," she says. "Let's go back inside. We can still have our party."

***

IN SAWBUCK SANCTUARY, backfire collides with wildfire. Conjoined flames rise over one hundred feet into the sky and *Vulcan's Hearth* burns with the mythic force of its namesake. Then, as if exhausted by the effort, the fires begin to die down. Cotton looks on with his men. The moon is eclipsed by smoke, and embers dim and brighten in light winds as the land turns quiet. In Cotton's cave, an old bear succumbs to the smoke. But the rest tuck noses into his hide and use his broad back as a shield from the heat. These bears survive. The mule deer and coyotes, mountain lions and feral cats, badgers and bobcats scatter to backyards and parks, crossing highways and boulevards. Some will be captured. Some won't survive. A few will find their way back into the woodlands. Even fewer will find mates, reproduce, and teach what they have learned. The trees are dead, the brush and saplings incinerated.

But the fires have stopped.

Nothing remains for them to consume.

TAUROMAQUIA

SLIDING DOWN, his chest against the Andalusian's trembling front shoulder, Mariano Cebellos, also known as "the Indian," gripped the saddle horn and thrust his sword hilt-deep between the shoulders of the charging bull. The horse standing firm despite every natural instinct, the picador pressing hard against the horse for leverage, and the bull, back legs kicking high, head and horns lowered, and massive shoulders bulging, pushing on against the burn and hideous pain of a sword piercing deep inside, all perfectly balanced in a horrible, beautiful dance.

I stared hard at the Goya etching. The finely rendered lines and strong composition, the dust and shadow, the delicate, precarious balance. Kathy took my arm and we walked on through the museum. The paintings and sculptures, the ancient masks and ceremonial dresses, the bones and the ruins: walking slowly from art to artifact, we eased through the sterile, marble corridors like pilgrims. At a circular open-air courtyard within the museum we stopped to smoke. I pulled out a pack and drew the last cigarette.

"Looks like we have to share." I said.

"That's fine. Just don't slobber all over it." Kathy made a phony grimace.

"I'll try," I said as I struck a match.

I lit the cigarette and took the first drag, passing it on to Kathy as I exhaled. Her hair and my smoke swirled around her eyes in the shifting breeze, her crimson silk shirt flapping and curling while we sat in silence. Kathy and I had been together for over a year now, a record for me, but we tried not to talk about the future. A Native American sculpture watched the sky above the courtyard. Spear and eyes raised, his feathers and bones rested steady on his enormous chest while the museum curled around us like an ancient blanket. We continued to pass the cigarette back and forth as if it were a sacred ritual pipe, the pattern of columns and shadows seeming to stare down on us, waiting, anticipating some sort of spectacle.

***

I WAS STRETCHING CANVASES at a local art shop in Savannah when I met Kathy. My scholarship covered tuition for a master's program in painting, but living expenses were left to me. Kathy was part-time at the shop, Make Your Mark Art Supplies, when I started. As an undergraduate art major, she took the job for the discount, her dreams of becoming an accomplished artist as strong as mine. When I first saw Kathy at the shop, she was stacking and labeling gesso, her straight sandy blonde hair, forever falling from behind her ears, becoming entangled in the tags. In her crouch, the back of her jeans bowed out, exposing the small of her back and giving the illusion of nakedness. I tried to focus on making forty-five degree cuts in my wood frames. Pulling her hair behind her ears, Kathy arched her back and a flash of red panties grabbed my attention. I was hypnotized after she left, the red crescent replaced with neatly stacked jars of gesso, stacked like seating rows in a Spanish arena, the Madrid Plaza, possibly the Zaragoza. It was several seconds before I realized I had cut my hand and stared stupidly at the trickle of blood falling on sawdust.

We started dating a few weeks later, my hand still showing a thin white line of scar tissue. We talked about art and movies on our breaks between work and classes, the park warm and sunny, the fountain blowing big beautiful bubbles from detergent —an adolescent prank, a dare maybe- percolating like children's babble behind our conversation. We went out for drinks and music at night, the long shadows cast from the moon and distant drums and chords accompanying us on our walks home, cobblestone clicking beneath our feet.

"It's beautiful out!" Kathy said. She took my hand and began swinging our arms in unison. "Where to, Mr. Lamb?"

"How about your place?" I said and smiled as our swinging arms turned into spins and skipping feet. Kathy hopped up on a long street bench and skirted the ridge of the backrest light like a tightrope, keeping the pace and hopping down to rejoin me. I had watched her leap from the tip of a rock face once, three or four stories high, and gasped as the brilliantly clear water swallowed her up in a mist of bubbles, translucent pearls softening her fall. Clamoring down through loose rocks and thorns, I emerged to find her splashing and giggling, euphoric from the rush of adrenaline. And I looked at her now, sea green eyes flickering in the lamplight, cadmium red paint stains on her dancing hands, and did my best to keep up. The bottom half of the moon reflected brightly in the sky, obscuring the stars around it, and was mimed endlessly by a line of overhanging street lamps. Moist air clung to our skin in the cool spring night, and a pair of owls hooted in the canopy of a nearby oak.

"This street reminds me of your painting," I said. "The guitar player."

"The lightning," Kathy replied, "And the way it makes the cobbles look wet."

"That's it," I said and slipped my arm around her waist.

"So am I going to see your art?" she asked.

"As soon as I do something you like."

Returning home from the museum, Kathy asked me if I thought I could have lived among the Indians, a culture of nature and sharing, of gods and circles, of spears and war-paint.

"I don't know," I said. "The Native Americans had a beautiful culture and a truly inspiring philosophy." Speaking like our tour guide, low and overly articulate, I held up my hands and curled my fingers, framing my museum voice in quotation marks. "The unique facets of tribal life are endless."

"But that's romanticizing," I said, speaking normally again. "I mean, I bet living in a tepee sucked. No heat, no A/C, and flies buzzing around your head. You know, like those cows on your aunt's farm. And what about chucking your spear at a buffalo while you're *trying to ride your horse*? Jesus, I don't know. Did you see how big those spears were? Damn!"

"If I could go back," Kathy started. "If I could live with a Hopi tribe, Pawnee, or Oglala Sioux, maybe I would. Kathy had emphasized Oglala and laughed. We made a game of pronouncing all the Indian names in the museum, and Oglala became our favorite. The *lala* in it sounded so childlike, we repeated it endlessly.

"If you spent your life like that," Kathy continued. "If you had grown up with the hunts and ceremonies," she switched over to her own museum voice. "Torturous sun dances and healing sweat baths, the Tirawa and the Wakan Tanka, I think it would be the most natural thing in the world."

Kathy leaned back in the car seat, pulled her hair behind her ears, and gave a quiet sigh before adding, "I could kill a buffalo."

I pulled into the gravel drive and parked. I was pretty much living at Kathy's full-time now, retreating to my own apartment for the privacy to paint, but spending nights and weekends here. I walked out onto the deck and Kathy, who had run in to put on her new souvenir –a relic, Native American Chants, and walked barefoot and clung to me at my waist. We held each other, swaying back and forth in each steady wind, chimes adding layers to the distant chants and tom-tom drum beats, high grass swirling in the yard beneath a low, red sun.

✱✱✱

KATHY'S PARENTS LIVED ON THE EDGE OF TOWN,

and her mother invited us to dinner on a regular basis. They owned a manor-style house of cut-stone firmly planted in a grove of massive oaks. In the winter, when the leaves were gone and the sky was gray, the house appeared castle-like, rigid and stoic. But now, in the late spring, serpents of ivy crawled all over the house, and while they could not penetrate the hardness of the stonework, the ivy seemed to soften the hard lines and edges and allow the manor to absorb some of the warm sunlight filtering in through the loose fabric of oak leaves. But even with the ivy, the house looked as if it could withstand anything.

Having taken her final undergraduate exam, Kathy drove us to her parent's house for a small graduation party. A few relatives and close college friends arrived early to help with the preparations and get a head start at the open bar. Mr. Dobbin, Kathy's stepfather, who had moved the family east after the wedding, cleared antiques and hand woven rugs from the den to make room for drinking and dance, flowers and balloons. Mr. Dobbin hated me. At first I just sensed it, like when you know someone is staring at you, even though you can't see them. Kathy assured me that he treated all of her boyfriends badly, but when I kept Kathy out all night over last year's Christmas Break, my suspicions held. Jack Gallop, a close friend of mine who was gaining quite a reputation as a local golfing champ as well as for having a new young female on his arm at every awards ceremony, played an instructional round with Mr. Dobbin the next day and called me that afternoon. *I waited up all night, they never called.* Jack did a fine impression, nasally monotone with just a hint of English accent. *She lives on her own now, but when she's home… in my house… The kid is no good, those ridiculous dreams of making a living as an artist. Why can't Kathy date someone with maturity?* What Mr. Dobbin meant to say was money, and I didn't have it.

Kathy's real father, Jesse Cossack – a broad shouldered log-buyer for a timber company- had been killed shortly after her birth. He had traveled out on horseback in Southwest Montana, elk hunting, when his horse reared at a black bear protecting her cub-filled den. In a spine-snapping fall, Jesse lay in a heap before the growling bear. His gun out of reach, his legs useless as bread dough, Jesse pulled out his knife and fought as best he could. Mr. Dobbin, however, was a legal consultant for a marketing company, and could not understand why Kathy had inherited all of her father's cowboy toughness, especially in such a thin and innocent shell. He pulled out a Wedgewood china serving bowl, a limited edition piece with a hand-painted gold leaf American Winery Guild's logo at its center, and placed it carefully on a maple serving table. As the preparations were made, and the drinking continued, hordes and expensive bottles of wine gathered around the china bowl like an attentive audience. Mr. Dobbin, growing weary of the high pitched giggles of half-drunk college girls, escaped to his study.

Mrs. Dobbin, however, was keeping up with the college crowd just fine, drinking wine and laughing loudly. She was as youthful at fifty as Kathy was now, and looked as if she could have been in the same graduating class. Her hair, forever falling from behind her ears, was sandy blonde, like Kathy's, but Mrs. Dobbin, Sarah, was not half as headstrong. Sarah had married Mr. Dobbin just two years after Jesse's death. Fearful, a child alone without any real income, Mr. Dobbin, who was a decent enough man, offered a great deal of security. Sarah had missed Jesse tremendously, and still did, but made certain that raising Kathy was her number one priority. At night, when Kathy was a little girl, Sarah had tucked her in tight with her stuffed bull, Ferdinand, and told her endless stories about Jesse, his strength, his dependability, his fantastic tales and his bad jokes, his love. With her bedtime stories, Sarah infused Kathy with Jesse.

Stepping up onto the cut-stone front porch of the Dobbin home, I stopped Kathy from opening the door. Danceflies buzzed in and out of the shaded ivy, and I could hear the muffled sounds of music and laughter inside.

"Before we go in," I said, "I'd like to give you something."

"Uh-oh, what did you do?" Kathy asked, rolling her eyes in feigned disinterest and grinning.

I produced a package from behind my back, a Whitman's sampler, and sheepishly held it out.

"Chocolate?" Kathy gave me a funny look followed quickly by an uneven smile.

"Thanks Ben. I, um, love chocolate…" The words were purposely raised in pitch.

"Have some."

"Maybe after the party."

"*Have some.*"

On opening the box, Kathy's face went blank, followed shortly by one raised eyebrow. Then, after a long confused second, she smiled, bouncing now and hair falling everywhere. Kathy retrieved the bone choker that has been snaking through the assorted candies. The carved buffalo bones were stacked three-high, linked with decorated leather straps between. In the center, the part that rest in front of her Adam's apple, was a flat, oval piece of bone with a diamond shape painted on it.

"The diamond shape is the Native American symbol for a feather," I said in my museum voice. "It is given to a warrior after doing something brave, *counting coup* for example. I saw you looking at it in the gift shop, and the lady said it was real, even the buffalo bones." I stopped and focused on her. "I'm so proud of you, Kathy."

"Thank you, Ben," she said, taking my hand and squeezing before letting go to pull her hair back into a pony-tail. "I love you too."

"Well," I said, shoving my hands into my pockets. "I guess we can go in now."

✳✳✳

WHEN I WAS A BOY, my father, James Lamb, took me hunting for White-tail in lower Alabama with a few of his hometown friends. We met up with his old gang in Jackson and followed each other on a ritual pilgrimage, our trucks and cars a gypsy caravan. The burnt-orange dirt roads wound endlessly through pine stands and quaint country cottages until we finally reached the camp house, nestled on the edge of a sprawling lake, dead cypress trees and Spanish moss, red-headed woodpeckers and enormous, gliding alligators.

The first night consisted mainly of heavy drinking and thick smoke, low-stakes poker and exaggerated hunting stories —and me, watching attentively between the spine and frame of the bunk room door, adding to my list of dirty words, bundled in a blanket. The men roared and howled at each other, calling bets and rattling glasses, and I wondered if that was what it meant to be a man. In spite of headaches and hangovers, everyone pulled themselves out of bed before sun-up, dressed in heavy layers, long-johns and sweaters, with camouflage suits on top, and piled into the twenty year old rusted truck to trek down to the belly of the swamp. My father and I were dropped off together, an expired license plate nailed to a tree marked the spot, and we marched quietly into the cold dark woods, shotguns on our shoulders, to our stand. Sitting there in the bitter cold darkness, listening to the rustling and moaning swamp, I was very afraid. My father, who had stayed up drinking, swapping lies was nodding off now, his back against an old oak, his shotgun across his lap. I looked down at my own shotgun, a fifteen year old Remington double-barrel –three years my elder, and gripped it fearfully at every hoot-owl and acorn fall. I could not imagine pulling the trigger.

The swamp was alive, cold and frightening, and as the sun began to cut slanted rays through the mist and trees, I was horrified to make out an immense, dark creature, grunting and stomping, white tusks becoming visible in the increasing light. Stories of the charging wild boar reeled back through me, men mimicking panic before the flickering hearth, shadows falling like giants all over the room. Sweating and shaking, I elbowed my father, passed out cold, and panicked when I didn't rouse. The boar rooted in acorns and mud thirty yards away, bulging shoulders and white tusks, grunts that sent a bitter cold to the nape of my neck. I lifted my shotgun, shaking and bleary-eyed, and tried desperately to aim the swaying Remington that seemed now to weigh an impossible ton.

"GODDAMN, GODDAMN BOY!!! WHAT? WHAT?" My father shot out in terror. "And what in the hell are you doing in my lap?"

By now the boar was hundreds of yards away –shoulders and hooves pumping, and birds were settling back down, the last fragments of oak bark twirling and drifting to the ground beneath the gaping scar that would mark the tree forever. I cowered in my father's lap, knocked there by the recoil of the gun, stuttering and choking my breaths, embarrassed and afraid, and even then, even at twelve years old, I somehow knew that a rite of passage had come and gone.

***

KATHY OPENED THE DOOR to squeals and shouts, wine glasses and hugs, sweet smelling perfumes and jazz. We moved into the den,

Kathy exchanging smiles and giggles with near teary eyes. *We'll keep in touch though. We'll write. You'll see, we'll always be friends.* I moved to the serving table, refilled my glass with Clarete, a dry Spanish red, and watched Kathy float through friends and family with charge and energy: an actor in the spotlight, ready for her audience, ready for the show. Pointing at her neck, I could see Kathy relating the story of my gift and the giving, looking up shiny-eyed and winking at me, and I knew I was completely in love.

Mrs. Dobbin came to the table to refill her own glass. Smiling and straightening my collar, she told me I looked handsome and complimented Kathy's gift.

"It was very nice of you to get her something," Sarah said.

I replied, "I thought it was her style."

"It certainly is that. It's very nice Ben." Sarah took a long drink of wine. "You know, Mr. Dobbin and I got Kathy something too."

"Great," I said. "What'd you get?"

"Well, it's…" Sarah took another drink of her wine. "Well, Mr. Dobbin will bring it out. Speaking of, where did my husband run off to?"

Topping of her glass, Sarah scurried out of the den to look for Mr. Dobbin. Finishing my own wine and beginning to feel the alcohol, I stared at an old family picture of Kathy and Mr. Dobbin. Kathy at seven years old, hair so blonde it looked white, straddling Mr. Dobbin's knee with a determined look on her face and digging her heels into his left calf as if to spur him on, faster and faster. Mr. Dobbin, who looked as old then as he does today, gave a manufactured smile, sallow complexion and darkened disks visible behind his eyeglasses, hands securely gripped around Kathy's waist. I refilled my glass and made my way back into the mingling crowd.

I was talking to one of Kathy's classmates about the Goya exhibit, particularly the way he presented the bullfight as beautiful and polished, tragic and horrible, when I caught a glimpse of Mr. Dobbin peering into the den, cheeks flushed with alcohol.

"Some of the etchings expressed empathy for the bull," Hunter said. "The one with the bull in the stands, with the dead guy hanging from his horns, that one was sick."

"That was one of the best," I said. "I loved it. And besides, you had to get off on seeing *the bull* win for once."

"No," Hunter miffed. "That's not what bullfighting is all about. It's a very specific tradition. In Tauromaqia, the bull dies."

Clinking a spoon against his wine glass, Mr. Dobbin asked for our attention, fully in the den now and holding an envelope with a bright red bow wrapped around it.

"I would like to congratulate all of our graduates tonight," Mr. Dobbin announced, "But there is one graduate I need to single out. Kathy, could you come up here?" he said, Sarah standing by his side and smiling. "We have something for you."

Kathy mazed through her friends to her parents, her hair tight in a pony-tail and stood beside them. As everyone was fairly drunk, no one noticed how long they stood there, the threesome hanging in some sort of paralysis: Mr. Dobbin, red faced and eyes glazed, Sarah wearing her smile like a politician, and Kathy, waiting in uncertain anticipation.

"Here you are, honey," Mr. Dobbin said. My eyes followed the red bow as it glided, slow motion, into Kathy's hands. Kathy looked across the room to me, smiled and winked, and tore open the envelope.

"A ticket to Paris?" she looked up, in obvious confusion. "What is… where is… the art program?" Kathy now began to piece things together and beamed. Kathy was bouncing now, hugging her parents like a child. She had applied to several programs abroad, but had thought she wouldn't get in. *I wouldn't want to leave anyway,* she had told me. *Things are good here, Ben. I'm happy.*

"I've taken a sabbatical from work," Mr. Dobbin said. "For six months, your mother and I will be able to travel and tour Europe while you begin your studies. We'll use Paris as home base."

"This is amazing!" Kathy blurted out. "Paris!"

I made my way back to the serving table and guzzled another glass of wine, drunk now and angry as hell about everything. Mr. Dobbin, red-faced and smiling genuinely, slid his arm around Sarah and whispered in her ear. I stared at the photograph again, Kathy on Mr. Dobbin's knee, and me swaying badly. I grabbed the table for balance. The serving table, antique and fragile, quivered and groaned before giving way under my weight. Finger foods and expensive wine crashing down, I barely noticed the sound of the Wedgewood china breaking my fall, priceless fragments flying. I felt it though, a shard of china passing through my shirt like rice paper. And as I lay there, drunk and spinning, bone white china fragments, Spanish red wine, and blood all mixed up on the split brick floor, I thought about Goya's etching of Mariano Cebellos: the picador supported by the strong andalusian, the bull dying from the sword in his back, and me, lying in my own blood, humiliated, defeated, and too drunk to get up.

But I did eventually get up, Kathy grabbing my hand and lifting, Sarah applying peroxide and bandages, and Mr. Dobbin quietly collecting the pieces of his limited edition bowl. Lubricated by alcohol, the party resumed its initial momentum. Later that night, after the party and the tearful goodbyes, Kathy and I sat out on her porch in a chair swing, full moon shining down and the first mayflies beginning their evening hatches, and I took her hand in mine.

"I'm sorry about tonight," I said, still drunk. "I'm happy for you though, going to Paris and everything. Shit, Kathy, Paris."

"It's ok, it was a surprise for me too." She reached for my bandaged back, and paused before continuing. "Are *you* ok?"

"I'm fine Kathy," I lied. "But I'll miss you when you are gone."

"I'll miss you too, Ben."

And so we sat swinging, watching the mayflies silhouetted by the moon, listening to chimes playing quietly, and Kathy, who had drawn the last cigarette from the pack, passed it on to me. Our smoke swirling and Kathy's silk shirt flapping and curling in the slow breeze, we passed the cigarette back and forth as ritual. And as we continued to swing, I let go of Kathy's hand, shifting uneasily from the pain in my back, and I knew that the dance was over.

TREASURE

THE BOX WAS HOT AND RUSTED. I turned it over in my hands, the iron hinges squealing, the fragile flakes of rust chipping off and spiraling to the soil. I looked inside, and, nesting cozy with folds of preserved silk and linen, lay the most hideous thing I had ever seen. I shut the box violently, snapping the lid down on escaping fabric and caustic malodor, red silk pinched tight while I refastened the clasp. I tucked the box under my arm like a football and sprinted down the trail through haunting pines and cedar trees, rain falling hard through gaps in the canopy and streaming down my shoulders and back. The trail was littered with roots, vines, and dead fall, but I hurdled and side-stepped, spun and twisted, and fast as a spooked deer, made the road into town.

*****

DURING THE SCHOOL YEAR I lived in Mobile, Alabama, a bustling coastal town, but in the summers I took a bus two hours north to stay at Grandpa's farm in Big Bend. One of the main reasons I looked forward to those summer months was March Florentine. March was just a year older than me, the daughter of Mario and Celia Florentine, who ran the farm down the road from Grandpa's place. She knew all the best swimming holes, the fastest shortcuts, and could easily knock a coke can off a log with a slingshot at fifty feet. I always looked for March through the tinted Plexiglas of the bus when I finally arrived, scooting up to the edge of my seat, my breath fogging up the glass, my hands nervous and squirming like caterpillars on newly exposed, white thighs. Inevitably she would appear, blonde hair whitening and green eyes squinting in the Alabama sun, cut off jeans, and a striped tank top exposing thin freckled shoulders. On afternoons after chores, March and I would jump and run from burly pirates, our secret mission to retrieve the treasure chest, ripe with gold and silver bullion, and return it safely to our invisible hideout. We would dive headfirst into Stripling Lake and throw water balloons at cars from red clay bluffs. And eventually, as the drowsy sun lay down at the edge of corn and cotton fields and the mosquitoes began to bite at our sunburned and dirty skin, we would migrate home, parting ways at rusting mailboxes, fingers untangling as our feet patted barefoot to separate paths.

The summer before, when I was twelve and March thirteen, our relationship had taken a slightly awkward turn. It wasn't that our friendship was flagging; it was just that March was acting different, brushing her hair different. She wasn't wearing makeup yet, thank God, but wearing her clothes different, sitting different, and worst of all, wearing a bra.

"Over the shoulder boulder holder," I rhymed. "Only you don't have any boulders."

"You wait until next year," March said. "then you'll see."

"See what?" I picked up a rock and skipped it across the surface of the lake, ripples colliding between hops.

"Go to hell," March said, crossing her arms and walking away.

***

WHEN THE BUS PULLED INTO A&P this year, I searched the parking lot feverishly for March. Usually I could spot her even before the bus made the wide turn off the main road, but this year I only saw my grandfather, hands locked behind his back, standing as erect as in his Navy years–chest out, stomach in.

"Where's March?" I shouted at Grandpa as I jumped around through assorted suitcases and trunks looking for my bag.

"Throw your bag in the back and get in, Tripper," my grandfather and March were the only two in town who still called me that. "Hurry up now, I'll tell you on the way."

March Florentine ran away five days ago, I found out. My grandfather chewed out the story slowly, carefully. He was smoking a cigarette with his window cracked open, air conditioning blowing hard on my knees, and I wanted to ask a lot of questions, but I felt nauseous and kept staring vacantly out the window of the Ford pickup. We passed over the Tombigbee River on an old metal spanning bridge, the cool water making its lazy curve, and I spotted an alligator climbing out onto the bank and disappearing into the high grass and weeds. The ashtray, garbled with butts, jumped and shifted as we made the transition from bridge to pavement.

Grandpa told me about Celia crying in his kitchen, desperate for answers, and I imagined her trembling, holding vigil for her lost daughter in a blue nightgown, tears furrowing through cakey makeup, hands wrapped around a short glass with nothing but ice rattling inside. He also told me about her father, Mario, grinding up the roads day and night with Sheriff Glanson, searching for anything, and I could see them in my mind, spotlighting through sweet gum, as we drove to Grandpa's farm. I blinked, caught a smoke-filled breath, and all I could see was my pale refection hanging there in the dirty glass.

First thing in the morning, I remembered something. I leapt from the top bunk, threw on shorts, and bolted past Grandpa at the stove where bacon snapped and popped in the black iron skillet. I ran outside barefoot and shirtless across the lawn, hurdled Skinner's creek, and veered down the trail. Sharp rocks cut into my tender, wintered feet, but the thing I remembered urged me on. At the bottom of the hill, I turned off into thick underbrush at a hollow, moss covered stump. Now, new spring vines snaked between ferns and newborn sapling shoots and cut at my ankles and shins as I ran. The distinctly thick smell of virile soil, rich with decay, was overwhelming in the humid, morning air. Just before the land dropped again and became swamp, I scrambled up on a fallen swamp cedar, out of habit mostly, having grown tall enough to reach the lowest branch from the ground, and quickly climbed up to unbolt the bottom hatch of our invisible hideout.

Every year, the hideout looked a little smaller, a little closer to the ground. Inside, the plywood floor was covered with blankets and sheets, and a hand-sewn crimson quilt my grandmother had made–given to March the year she was born– wound in a spiral at the center, as if by a visitant dog turning circles before bedding down. Radiating out from the quilt, the fort was littered with trash: coke cans, snack wrappers, magazines, empty cans of Raid, paper plates, plastic utensils, and dirty clothes. Our pirates' gold, a handful of leftover Mardi Gras coins, shined dully in loose constellations. A dark knot of towels sopped in the corner. Above the mess on the floor, a square hole had been cut into the sturdiest wall, and a cross-shaped frame of cotton gum branches was glued to the center. White linen napkins draped from thumbtacks completed the picture window, pink ribbons pulling them aside in soft, fluttering curves. The window gave view to the swamp, water elms, and cypress trees wading quietly in murk and rot.

On top of a rotten milk crate, a yellow envelope sat pressed between the blade and handle of our folding trowel. My name was etched neatly across it in black ink, my full name: George M. Bedford III. I snatched up the envelope, ran my finger through the gummy seal, and unfolded the single sheet of thin yellow paper.

Dear Tripper,

Sorry I missed you this year, but lots of stuff happened since you been gone. I have gone to hide out at the beach. You can't tell NO ONE!!!! I ain't coming back for a long time. If I see your house down there, I will put a letter in the mailbox. I have only seen it in pictures, so I might not know which one it is.

March

PS. I borrowed the treasure chest. Don't be mad.

I shoved the letter into my pocket and squeezed out of our hideout, ferreted down to the swamp cedar and leapt off, my legs twisting in the air even before touching the ground. I sprinted the trail and pounded numb feet back to the farm.

When I returned, Grandpa was sitting with Sheriff Glanson, sipping coffee and smoking. Glanson was an old friend of Grandpa's from their Navy days. His graying hair and mustache bristled like a grooming brush and his heavy frame spilled out from the white pine kitchen chair. "Grandpa, I think I know where March is," I announced, breaking up their conversation.

"So do we," Glanson said.

"Huh?"

"You missed breakfast, Tripper." Grandpa said.

"We picked her up last night," Glanson continued, grinding out a cigarette. "She was clear down to Minnow Bay, trying to hitch a ride further south."

"She's alright now, Tripper." Grandpa reached out a twitching hand to my shoulder. "She's home safe with her mamma and pop." I could smell moonshine through the coffee on Grandpa's breath. I put my hand in my pocket with the letter, rubbing the thin, smooth paper with my fingers.

"Now wash up and get your breakfast."

"I'm not hungry," I said.

"I made breakfast and you're gonna eat it! Now you wash yer hands and eat that goddamned breakfast you little..."

I didn't hear the rest. When the swinging door shut behind me, the words became muffled and distorted. I went out the front door and skirted that edge of the yard, darting out of sight onto the path to the Florentine farm.

***

AFTER GLANSON FOUND HER, March wouldn't come out of her house for days. I went over and knocked on the door every afternoon after chores, but Celia would only say that she was resting and that I should give her time. So I began going back out to our hideout. I went back and began cleaning. I collected all of the trash, scooped it into a bag, and hiked it out to the dumpster behind our A&P grocery. I slung all the blankets over my shoulder and took them home while Grandpa was out, washing them in the claw-footed bathtub, returning the crimson quilt Grandma had made to Celia. I swept out the floor with clumps of olive pine needles, and I stole a combination lock from our trunk in the attic for the bottom hatch. The only thing left, the thing I had been avoiding every day, was to get rid of the dark stained towels. I knew it was blood, I had known right away, but something inside me was unwilling to think about what that meant. I buried the towels at the edge of the swamp, scattering leaves and branches over the disturbed earth, and then clicked the lock shut, one hand clutching the lock itself, the other spinning the memory of the combination away.

***

THE WEEKS OF SUMMER CRAWLED ON, and March remained holed up in her room. A drought was steadily burning up the crops, zero precipitation for the month and two inches behind, but worse, six inches behind for the year. No rain was forecast. Grandpa and Mario never had the money to put in the elaborate watering system that some of the other farms relied on, and they watched helplessly as their investment began to wither and brown. In early mornings they had begun channeling water from Skinner's Creek into the fields, but it wasn't enough. The temperature rising with the sun was incapacitating, a hundred and ten degrees, and by midday we all huddled in the kitchen with box fans, glasses of coke, and damp rags. In late afternoon, when the air would become heavy and thunder would throw teasing rumbles across the fields, I started heading back to the woods.

Smoking cigarettes I had slipped from Grandpa's carton, I retraced all of the paths March and I had worn through the trees. I went to Skinner's Creek, Stripling Lake, and the red clay bluffs and rotting swamp. I walked the dusty gravel roads and the dirt paths, sputtering my breaths when trying to inhale. I even caught myself playing one of our old childhood games, running and jumping from pirates, searching for our lost gold. But this time I decided to become a pirate myself, squinting to look tough, lighting a stolen cigarette, and mapping out possible burial sites for the bullion. I threw rocks and dirt clods at the invisible hideout, yelling threats and obscenities through the shroud of leaves, proclaiming my evil plans.

There were several places that March and I had buried the treasure chest. Some of them we had used frequently, but most were just random clearings in the woods, magical patches of soft earth and sunlight. I went through the common ones right off, digging a few inches down and deciding by the feel of the soil that no one had been there recently. Then I fanned out to more obscure spots, but found only worms and roots, rusty cans and roly polys, centipedes and slugs. For a few days I abandoned the search to go swimming, the lake water so warm from the heat.

But one afternoon, with a darkening sky overhead, I left Grandpa sitting expectantly on the porch, eyes turned up to the pregnant clouds, and I went back to the trails. The air hung rippled with electricity. As I walked, I thought about March. I had been thinking about her every day, wondering if she would ever, ever come out, but today I thought about years past, about the times we'd played together, and about the times we'd held hands. And of course, I thought about the end of last summer, when we'd started to watch each other change after swimming, and for the first time I wanted to kiss her, her white blonde hair pulled back behind her ears and her tan freckled shoulders and her breasts beginning to show. And then that night just before I went home, the first and only time March and I spent an entire night together in the hideout, when we tried out all sorts of things. I wondered if my freewheeling sense of exploration that night had something to do with this nightmare we were now in.

I ended up at the hideout as the thunder began in earnest, rolling out in the distance like a train. I knew I couldn't open the lock I had attached to the hatch, so I climbed out limb over limb, making my way above the hideout walls. From there I shimmied out over the skylight, a gap between boards we used as a roof, and from there, I lowered myself in. Everything inside was as I had left it, and I sat down next to March's makeshift window, staring out. The edge of the swamp had receded fifty yards in the drought and a skeletal root system was left exposed. Raindrops began to patter on the roots and dry ground, sucked up and swallowed as they hit. And then I saw it. Pushing my face into a corner of the window, I could see the top half of our treasure chest, wedged into a clutch of cypress roots.

Knowing how much harder it was to climb out of the skylight than to climb in, I started kicking at the bottom hatch with my heels. The wood was bruising and needling splinters into my bare feet. Thunder rumbled closer now and rain began to come through the skylight on my back, head, and shoulders. One heavy kick with my weight behind it and the hatch popped open, the lock and hinge dangling useless from the also dangling hatch, blood smeared across the pine, and me, born helpless through the hole and crying out as I crashed from cedar to dirt. And the dirt stuck to my body, wet with sweat, blood, and rain, while I gasped and wheezed, trying to regain my breath. Pulling myself up, I stood dazed, wiped off my eyes with the back of my hand, and walked through the strengthening rain to the box, our treasure chest.

I was halfway to town when I stopped running, my heart and lungs shuddering and heaving, the rain steady and lighting crackling across the sky. I walked a few minutes, catching my breath and passing the silver guardrail, until I came to the middle of the bridge and stopped. Pulling the box from under my arm, I placed it on the wet, metal railing and looked out at the water elm and cypress trees, the possum oak and pine, with limbs gently reaching out over the river like outstretched hands. Looking down at my own hands, I realized they had grown. They were as large and strong as any man's. The quiet clay banks guided the amber water, beginning to swell and quicken with rain, along the curving course of the Tombigbee. I watched a lone alligator, seeming to guard the river itself, and took the chest back into my hands. It seemed that the chest suddenly weighed a hundred pounds for all it contained. Rain hung heavy in my bangs. And as I threw the chest over the rail and into the river, I could hear my grandfather's songs, deftly picked melodies in my head. I stood erect, chest out, stomach in, on a metal spanning bridge with rippled water pulsing beneath, and allowed those songs to radiate across my body. The notes were pure and true.

DOG DECISION

THE BAR FIGHT HAD BEEN SHORT-LIVED, but violent. One man sat in the corner with a bag of ice on his jaw. Two others had been wheeled off to the Baptist hospital in an ambulance. It was quiet in the bar. I washed the torn skin from my knuckles carefully in the men's room, and they were already turning dark as thunderheads. The young waitress brought me another scotch. I paid, gulped it down, and walked to my truck. I thought about the way my wife Jessica hated it when I drove home from a bar, her hair falling in a raven frame around her face, her hands curled up on her belly like a sleeping kitten.

There was a note on the door at my home in the valley. "Gone to Amy's til this storm blows over. I'll call tonight. – Jess." I ripped the note down and went inside, out of the wind. Shakes licked my battered hand, wagging his tail with a slow rhythm. His dish sat empty. I pulled the fresh bottle from the bag, poured half a glass, and gave Shakes some dry food. The scotch was numbing and I could feel it tingle in my cheeks. My eyes grew as heavy as they tend to do when rain taps on the roof. Jess and I used to sit up late on rainy nights in t-shirts and robes and try to pick out tunes, rhythmic melodies, in the delicate tapping. Sometimes I really thought I could hear those songs dancing on the roof, and thus, in our ears. I sat in the leather chair by the phone and had another drink.

***

"HELLO..." I GRUMBLED, fighting cobwebs in my head.

"Ben, are you asleep?"

"No, no..." I lied. "Just tired."

"Well I..."

"Are you feeling ok, Jess?" I interrupted.

"I'm fine," she quickly stammered. "How's Shakes? Does he miss me?"

"Of course he does, don't you Shakes?" I look over to Shakes sleeping on his bed, tail curled in, front paws tucked under his chin. "Shakes says you need to come home."

"What are you going to do, Ben? Can you get another job?"

"I haven't lost my job yet."

"Come on, Ben, you know you can never go back there. They've seen you all over the news. They think you are some sort of angry activist, and they don't like the attention." Her voice was less sympathetic now, and something deep inside me began to knot up.

"Do you think I wanted this? Do you think I wanted a fight? Come on, Jessica." I became louder now and my booze swam to my head.

"Yes, because you didn't get one from me."

I eased up and shifted my weight from one side to another. "You wouldn't even discuss it."

"I'll call back tomorrow. Sober up."

***

I AWOKE FROM EMPTY DREAMS and stiffly walked from the den to the kitchen. It was colder in the mornings now. Shakes bounded to the back door and urgently wagged his tail. I opened the door for him and started to make coffee. My head pounded. My hand looked like hell. It was strange the way the scabs were under my knuckles, not right on them. I assumed the friction from the angle of the punch stretched the skin prior to tearing it. The caller-ID on the counter

105

showed three calls this morning that I had not heard. All from Ann's in Portland. I drank my coffee and walked outside to throw Shakes a tennis ball and smoke a cigarette.

A call had come in from the office. *Termination effective immediately.* I walked back outside and continued throwing Shakes a ball. He wasn't the most well trained dog, but Shakes loved to fetch and could give affection like no other. It was as if the ball came alive for him every time; a new game every single time. The phone rang, and Shakes sat at my feet, looking up in anticipation. I sat down and gave Shakes a scratch, then tossed the ball. The phone stopped ringing. The valley was quiet. With Jess gone and no job to go to, I sat in a clouded daze. My life had come to a standstill, teetering between two distinct fronts. On one was my old life. The steady job, the wife, the cabin and the dog. The other was some strange void; one that I did not know how to fill. I could go either way. Retreating back inside, the soft leather chair cradled my body like an infant. Shakes lay at my feet.

I called Kevin from the bar. I asked if I could come see him outside of town and he said sure. He asked if Jessica was coming. When I said no, he sighed. The bar was loud and I told him I'd call when I got on his street.

The bartender, Pierre, was an old friend of mine from high school. His burly presence made him very, very good at his job. His hands alone were enough to make you think twice about pulling something stupid; big, scarred, violent hands. But he was a good friend, and though I'd seen him beat a man mercilessly once, none of the scars were from beating me. The valley had been my home. My tab was small, so I paid cash and left a generous tip, choosing to ignore the knot in my stomach from my loss of job. I knew Pierre had kids at home, sleeping and dreaming about backyard football with Dad in the crisp, fall air. I told him I'd be gone for a while and gave him Kevin's number; if he heard anything about the bar fight, I wanted to know. He said sure and shook my hand. I was always surprised at how gentle those hands could be.

"Get your shit together," Pierre said. "Get it together and come back home. Jessica needs you right now."

"She's fine, Pierre." I said. "But when she gets back, watch out for her just the same."

***

I DROVE INTO TOWN a bit after eleven while the wind whipped across the highway. The truck shifted in the wind and made me vaguely sick, vaguely feeling unsafe. I stopped for gas and called Kevin. He said to bring some beer and to come on. I bought a case of Budweiser, two packs of Marlboro's, and headed up the dirt road to his cabin. The lights were on and the dogs circled us barking, tails wagging, as I parked. Shakes joined right into the bark fest and I let him out to join the others.

Kevin greeted me on the porch. The smell of steaks and charcoal blew up from the grill. I wish I had come earlier. Kevin made a drinking sign with his hand, and crushed a cigarette under his boot. Kevin was an average sized man, his features unremarkable in any way. But as soon as he began to speak, his booming, articulate voice gave him a presence that demanded your attention.

"So what did you do this time, Ben?" Kevin asked as he took two beers from the case, and put the rest in the refrigerator.

Kevin and I talked until dawn and then stepped out to feed the dogs. Shakes jumped and snapped like a puppy, happy to be with the other dogs. Kevin gave them the moist, canned stuff and they wolfed it down greedily. A break in the clouds allowed a spotlight of sun to illuminate the fringe on Shakes' ears. Kevin leaned back against a tree while I sat on the steps. The dogs ate noisily between us. There was something about the dog's greedy happiness that I watched and felt pangs of longing for. As dogs, they had a community. They understood one another.

"So... What are you going to do?" Kevin lit a cigarette and shrugged his shoulders in disbelief.

"Well, there's Jess to keep in mind," I said. "I want to work things out with her. Hell, I *have* to works things out with her. But as for a job, or a new place to live, I just don't know. We could go anywhere, do anything. It is so open that I can't come up with anything at all," I paused and blew smoke into the wind.

"I hate to leave our valley, it's been our home, but I can't imagine staying now. Everything has changed. Come on, Shakes, lift those perky paws and tell me what to do."

"I can get you a job with the paper over here if you want. You've worked with those guys already anyway," Kevin raked his fingers through his hair. "Look, just do what makes you happy, Ben. The rest will follow the front."

I sat on the porch and could not stop watching the dogs. They had an unspoken language. But it was crystal clear who was in charge of who and what anyone wanted at any given time. The sun was hot, but a breeze kept me cool. The dogs continued to play, nipping each other and barking with excitement in the fall weather. They rolled in the leaves and pine straw. Clouds drifted across the sky, spotlighting different dogs with sun as they rolled by. After dinner and a couple of brews I thanked Kevin, called Shakes to jump in my truck, and drove back home.

Jessica was there when I arrived. Shakes ran to see her, overwhelming her with affection. I followed and gave Jess a hug. Awkward at best. Inside the cabin, I noted it was cleaner than I had left it. No bottles or glasses in my den. A newly knitted quilt lay across the leather chair.

Jessica scratched Shakes behind his ears. Shakes lay with his feet in the air in complete submission.

"I've missed you Ben," Jessica said.

"I've missed you too, Jess. This will all settle down."

"Are we going to be ok? Can we be now?" Jessica asked with a look of true concern.

"Of course we are fine," I replied smiling. "But I've been thinking we should move. Get a change of air. Too much old energy here."

"You have any ideas? Schemes, or what?" Jess asked and stepped closer to me.

"Well," I replied with a wide smile. "Shakes really seems to like it where Kevin lives. He has friends over there. Good ones. Don't you, boy?"

"You know I still feel the same way, don't you?" Jessica tapped her boot.

"Yep, and I feel the same too. But we have to move past this. The bar fight is over," I looked to the new quilt on the chair.

"I know," Jessica followed my eyes to the quilt. The look in her eyes told me she had made it.

"Let me tell you about the paper where Kevin is," I said.

Jessica and I stepped into the kitchen for coffee and talked about moving while the valley prepared for winter. Shakes watched and followed us. He wagged his tail.

FOUR DAY WORRY BLUES

ROUND 1:

I'M NAKED TO THE WAIST. The first blow comes in low and fast. I weave left, but his fist catches my right oblique. I spit blood onto bare feet and uppercut with my right. I miss. His jab catches my chin. The room blurs and I step back. The cross lands hard against my temple. I feel the wall at my back. I feel glass breaking against expensive art. I feel the floor rise up to my knees. Leaning forward, my sweaty fingers grab at the edge of the rug. The woolen threads feel soft. My face presses against hardwood and glass. I smell bourbon. The man buttons down his cuffs and leaves the room. It's our first living room, the one before all the divorces and the step-this and half-that. I have this dream every night. Sometimes the man is my father, sometimes it's Mason. Most times I can't see his face. Either way, we go at it bare knuckles. This morning, I wake up with bruised hands.

ROUND 2:

I DUCK DOWN, stepping back and blocking with my fists. He comes in fast. He lands two jabs, an uppercut, and finishes with a cross. I'm blinded by sweat and blood. I cover my face, peering between fingers. It's Dad tonight. No, now it's Mason. The dream is always like this. I shut my eyes.

***

MASON LETS ME STAY IN HIS ROOM the first night at the University. Dad forgot to send boarding fees. No one knows where he is. The guy assigned to live with Mason never shows up, so things work out. Mason and I have been best friends since middle school. His hair turned gray senior year, so I started calling him Governor. Then everyone did. It was as much for the hair as for his politics. He wants to be JFK. He keeps our room white-glove clean. Mason's father, who drove up for welcome weekend, gives Mason an Oxford English Dictionary. He wraps thick, hairy arms around our necks and says Sewanee will make men of us. I hear him remind Mason that his scholarship requires *at least* a 3.0. Mason reminds his father that he was valedictorian. The father gives Mason twenty dollars. Through the crack of the bathroom door, I watch them hug.

The dorm is coed. I walk the breezeway overlooking the courtyard. Heather steps out of her room in flip-flops with a towel over her shoulder.

"Have you taken the swimming test?" she asks.

Heather braids her ponytail and looks at me with huge green eyes. A black bathing suit shows through her t-shirt.

"A test?"

"The University says every student has to swim 50 yards." She spins goggles on a finger. "They don't want us to get drunk and drown in one of the lakes."

"Oh," I say. "I didn't know."

"The lakes are everywhere. Little death traps when they freeze under the snow."

"I swim all right."

"I'm going now. Wanna come?" Heather taps painted toes. She smiles.

"Sure. I think so. Is the test in a lake?"

"Of course not. The cold would kill you."

"But it's only September."

"Are you coming or not?"

ROUND 3:

I TRY A JAB-CROSS COMBO but the man is quick. The cross leaves me open and the man drives a straight to my ribs. I hear the stitching rip in his starched white shirt. I pull up, lift my fists. He uppercuts to my jaw. Blood fills my mouth. I can't catch my breath and I can't see clearly. The man turns blurry and his next hit lands across the bridge of my nose. I step back. I hold out my hands in surrender.

***

I'M PACKING FOR MONTANA. Dad said no, but I'm going. Heather's going too. My canvas bag looks like a split potato with clothes popping from the seam. I slide my fly rod into an aluminum tube and fill a plastic box with Pheasant Tails, Zug Bugs, and Hoppers. Mason comes in from a mid-term and sits on his bed. A poster of JFK is taped to the wall over his shoulder. Next to it, his autographed photo of George Stephanopoulos. Our beds lie four feet apart in this tiny dorm room. He rubs a hand under his jaw line.

"My throat is killing me."

"You probably pulled something studying last night. You should fix it up with a fifth of whiskey and dirty sex."

"Seriously, it hurts."

"All that reading will do you in."

"Grades equal money."

"How long has it hurt?"

"A week now. Are you going to hang that shirt up?"

"Does my nose look ok? Took a soccer ball in the face."

"I can't see anything."

"You should talk to the nurse about that throat."

"I'll see my doctor at home." Mason picks at the hem of his khakis.

"What about the beach?"

"Canceled."

"What?" I turn from my clothes and face him.

"I feel like shit."

"Shake it off. Be a man."

"Bite me."

Mason picks up my shirt and hangs it in the closet. He opens our mini-fridge and grabs a coke.

"Whiskey, Governor. Not coke. And I'm packing that shirt."

"I thought Montana was off?"

"Why don't you ever drink?"

"What about your Dad?"

"Who gives a shit. It's not like he'll remember in a week."

I turn back around, put my knee into the clothes, and press down hard enough to zip the bag. My ribs throb with pain.

ROUND 4:

HEATHER STANDS BETWEEN US. She lifts both arms, palms out. She pushes off my chest. I move back. But the man grabs her hand and twists Heather to the ground. I watch his boot twist into her shirt as he comes after me. I put everything into a straight and knock Dad's teeth out. But he gets up. He sits in a Windsor chair and gums a bloody cigarette. Heather disappears from the dream. It happens sometimes.

Dad says, "Got me good, did ya? But you'll never get away. Look at that hand." I look down at one of Dad's eye teeth jutting from my knuckle. I pick it out and toss it to him. In the dream, he pops it back in his mouth.

✳✳✳

ON THE EAST BANK of the Blackfoot river, Heather and I sit on a fallen hemlock. We've fished through the cold morning. Warm sunlight finally breaks over the tree line as I light two cigarettes. I pass one to Heather. She moves to the water's edge and balances at the edge of a flat rock. She flips up the creel lid and looks inside. Two browns and a brook trout slosh in the frigid water.

"Should we release them?" she asks.

"I thought they were dinner."

"We bought steaks."

"Fine by me."

Heather lifts trout one at a time. She cradles their slick bellies underwater until instinct reminds them to swim.

"We should get a dog," I say.

"What kind?"

"The big kind."

"Like a Boxer?"

"No." I rub my thumb against my index and middle finger. "Pound dogs are free."

"You worry so much about money."

"That's because I don't have any."

"You're rich."

"Dad is rich."

"What would we name it?" Heather throws the empty creel onto the bank and finishes her cigarette. She grinds the butt against a rock and thumps it at me.

"Blue," I say.

"Why Blue?"

"Why does he have to be such an asshole?"

"Booze." Heather pulls a six pack from the river. She hands me one.

"Blue is a good name for a dog." I drink from my beer. "So when are you going to ask me about the fighting?"

"What fighting?"

Patches of sunlight flit across my hands and the cuts are harder to see.

"Yeah," I say. "Blue."

ROUND 5:

THE MAN LANDS HIS FIRST PUNCH. I shake it off, skip right, and work a combination. My jab nicks his chin. He side-steps the cross. Then he lands three for three and I'm spitting blood. I try to call the fight, but my swollen tongue won't produce sound. I duck under the harvest table and stay to the shadows. Broken glass litters the cold floor. It smells like bourbon.

***

MASON'S NOT AT THE DORM when I get back, but the room is immaculate. I unzip my bag and throw every single piece of clothing on the floor. I check the machine. Two messages from Mom and then it's Mason: *Hey Ben. I'm still at home. I'm sure I'll be back in a day or two. How was fishing? Call me.*

I pick up the phone and dial.

"Governor."

"Ben."

"Got your message."

"Yeah. It's not good."

"What'd they say?"

"They did a biopsy on the lymph node in my neck. Hurt like god-almighty."

"Shit."

"It's Cancer."

I say nothing. I scratch at the back of my head and look around the room. Fishing gear on the bed, skis in the corner, and my bike hangs from the ceiling. Mason hardly owns a thing.

"Hodgkin's Disease. That's what they called it. Said it's treatable. No sweat."

I tap the phone against my ear.

"You still there?"

"Yeah. I'm here." I struggle for words. "Sorry, Gov."

"It's fine. I'm fine."

"I'll come down there. It's only a couple of hours."

"Seriously, I'm fine. How was fishing?"

I tap the phone against my ear.

ROUND 6:

I MOVE IN AND UPPERCUT to his stomach with my right. The man staggers back, bumping into the silver tea service and toppling the sugar bowl. He spits to the hardwoods. I see blood. He's angry now, but I still can't see his face. This time he throws a haymaker. I'm off my feet and falling fast.

***

DAD LEAVES THE CABARET. The highway is dark. He steers with his left hand and drinks '82 Lafite Rothschild from the bottle with his right. "Hothouse," he says. "Hell of a place." The wet blacktop glitters under stray pockets of lamplight. Dad finds the replay of the game on the radio. The Cubs are up by one at the top of the ninth. He listens to the Reds strike out as the right tires of the Mercedes stutter on center markers. The car drifts into the right lane. He taps his thumb against the steering wheel and closes his eyes. The shoulder gravel vibrates the car and Dad wakes. He overcorrects left. The car crosses both lanes and dips into the grass median, popping over the muddy ditch and climbing the other side. Dad looks into the glare of oncoming traffic as his car leaves the median. All four tires leave the ground. The Mercedes' front bumper hits first, shattering glass and bending metal on the rear door of a tan Buick. Both cars spin off the shoulder and into the weeds.

A highway patrolman is first on the scene. He calls in the ambulance and checks the Mercedes with a flashlight. Blood runs from Dad's forehead into his open mouth. He taps the steering wheel with his thumb.

"Hey hey, Cubbies," Dad says.

"Sir, are you all right?"

"Chicago wins again."

"Do you know where you are, sir?"

"I'm in Alafuckingbama you little shit."

"I see you've been drinking."

"The '82 is every bit as good as the '59."

"Don't move Sir, paramedics will be here soon. I need to check on the other car."

The patrolman jogs to the Buick. He checks with a flashlight. The woman in the driver's seat slumps forward. The child in the back screams. The patrolman feels for a pulse on the woman, then turns to wave the ambulance in.

At least, this is how I imagine it happened. I've talked to the cop. I feel sure I have it right.

ROUND 7:

I COME AT HIM SWINGING. I'm hyped up and punching hard. The man dances around my swings, grinning. He bobs side to side, then lands a cross to my jaw. The sting of it flicks a switch in my head and I rush him. I shove him to the ground and kick his ribs. The man curls into a ball. I kick his face and sides, the back of his head. I jump down and grip his shoulders. I spit in his face. The man keeps grinning as Heather pulls me off. Even this close, I have no idea who he is.

***

MASON LIES BACK IN THE ICU, head elevated by pillows. A ventilator breathes for him. Vaseline has been slathered in his eyes. I've been told it's a lose-lose situation. They can't treat the Hodgkin's for a virus in his heart and they can't treat the virus for the Hodgkin's. The waiting room is crowded with family and friends, but the doctor only allows us to say our goodbyes one at a time. Mason's sisters and mother talk us through it. The older sister says, "He can hear you, so say whatever you want." I don't know what to say. On the nightstand, the mother tears open a white sugar pack for coffee. Her hands tremble and less than half finds the cup. She tears into another. The younger sister looks up to me, then turns to Mason. She says, "Time to go play in the clouds, Bubba-cat." At this, the mother cries. I start to ask why she calls him Bubba-cat, but don't. I realize it's time. Mason's mother hugs me, but cannot speak. I stare over her shoulder at the spilled sugar. Mason's mother kisses my cheek. I move to the table and brush the granules into my hand. I make sure I get them all. Then I nod to Mason and step out through the curtain so the doctors can turn off the machines.

ROUND 8:

I LAND TWO JABS and a cross. The man takes one step back, then drives forward with a straight to my nose. I fall backward onto the antique butler's tray. Bottles of wine shatter under my weight. I look up from the floor and see the man picking through the shards. It's Dad. He lifts a piece with the label still intact and reads from it. "Intensely flavored with cassis, spice, and wood." He drops the glass and stands. He crosses his arms. Heather steps in from the kitchen and rushes over. She kneels in the wine and presses two fingers against my wrist. She's saying something, maybe even yelling, but I can only see her lips move and chin tremble. I can't hear a thing.

***

DAD GROPES THE SHEETS with shaking hands. He kneads folds of thin fabric, releases, then kneads again. Blood soaks through a bandage on his forehead where the '82 Rothschild pierced his skull. I'm the only one here. I sit on a metal folding chair and look at the dull monitor screen, blipping without rhythm. I glance at my hands, three band aids on the left, four on the right, then down to my leather boots. I bought the boots years ago. Just like Dad's. Same brand, same size. A scuff on the right toe matches one on the left heel where I kick them off. I dig the right toe in between the leather and sole, sending the left boot to the floor. Left boot, then right. Always in that order. Dad does the same. The monitor squawks and I look up.

"Horrible wreck," the doctor says. "He may not make it through the night."

I look at the doctor, expressionless, then back at my father. The tubes mumble and pulse. I can't think of anything to say, and instead, I begin to hum softly. My voice grows stronger as the humming becomes words. It's an old blues ballad by Blind Lemon Jefferson:

Just one kind favor
I'll ask of you

I sing loose and smooth, imitating Blind Lemon as best I can. The nurses peer at me with sidelong glances. They pretend not to notice.

One kind favor
I'll ask of you

I keep singing. I forget myself and sing loudly, loud enough that I think Dad might hear.

Lord, it's one kind favor
I'll ask of you

The monitor emits a constant beep that I remember from movies and dreams. I produce the last line with air from deep within my lungs.

See that my grave is kept clean.

The doctor moves to Dad and checks his pulse.

"Sorry," He says. The doctor clips the heart monitor back on to Dad's finger. "False alarm."

The machine resumes, even beeps.

"Fucking Christ," I say.

"These little clips are tricky." The doctor makes a routine check of vitals, and turns to me smiling. But then his face changes. His eyes open wide.

"You've got a hell of a nose bleed."

I look down at my shirt, my pants. Blood covers everything. I lift my head and hold my nose.

"Nurse," he says. "Bring me some gauze, a towel."

I stare at the ceiling.

"Don't worry son, your father's turned the corner. He's a real fighter."

"Christ," I say.

I ball my hand into a fist.

ROUND 9:

MASON GOES DOWN IN A SINGLE PUNCH, but I'm not sure I threw it. He falls back, opens his eyes and says, "Look at Bubba-cat now, he sure ain't the Governor." He won't get up. I scream at him to get to his feet, but he lies sideways on the floor. He reaches for a blanket on the couch and pulls it over his face. Tables, chairs, paintings, and lamps lie in pieces around the room. There is nothing left unbroken. Heather stands behind me, so I turn to her. She opens a new pack of cigarettes and pulls two out. She lights them with a match. Music begins to play from somewhere unseen, distant and muted. But it's enough. Heather drops the match into spilled bourbon as we walk through the door.

I say, "I've never left this room."

Heather says, "You have now."

***

I STAND OUTSIDE our crumble-stilts house, ten years since Mason died. Crickets edge between blades of grass, hidden, clicking and chirping the night song we all know. My toes yawn out, pressing into the cool and damp. Alabama moonshine falls across the lawn and my hands slip into cotton pajamas for a cigarette and match. Blue sniffs invisible trails, tail wagging and head down low. His muzzle turned gray last winter, and it's hard to believe we've had him this long. Heather drove us straight from the funeral to the pound. We sat on folding chairs in a little square room and a woman brought puppies to us, one by one. Blue had the biggest paws. Today is his birthday.

We've just moved in to this house. We've unpacked our boxes and we've done the cleaning. We do not feel like strangers in this house. My grandfather built it. The Childress River winds along the back yard and disappears south. Dad jaundiced when his liver gave way to tumors last year. He survived the wreck, but not the drinking. He left all his money to a wife somewhere, but we don't know her. Blue goes to the door and looks back to me. His shoulders sit almost as high as the doorknob.

Above Blue, I see Heather through the screen. She no longer smokes. It's harder for me.

The moon is closer to the Earth than usual. The night is clear and I look up at the craters, piecing together eyes and a mouth. I can't make out much of a nose, and only when I squint does he take an appropriate shape. In this light, my hands appear ivory white. No cuts, no bruises. Leadbelly calls out to me from our window. It's *Four Day Worry Blues*. I'm not sure if I'm awake, so I wiggle my toes. The grass feels real. Crickets drop layered chords into our song. I glance down at the silhouette of garbage at the curb, boxes and bags of Dad's clothes and cracked glasses. With all his belongings inside, the house felt cluttered and dirty. So I threw them out.

Looking back to the moon, I say, "Goodnight, Governor," and take a deep breath. I put out my cigarette and walk barefoot to the house. Blue follows me in. Heather is already asleep, and I slip into bed without waking her. I watch her eyes dart side to side under closed lids. It's warm here and I'm tired, so I make a fool's wish. I put an arm around Heather. I shut my eyes. I wish to sleep without dreaming.

LOVE

BEN AND HEATHER, they sure have moved around. But always, always do they reconnect. Heather and Ben. Ben and Heather. The real story, the one I've been skirting the edges of, is that Ben and Heather are the sort of soul-mates who go on to the next life together. They are born, live and die, are reborn, and die again, and still they hold hands. They are connected in ways that Ben did not realize this go around, what with all the other women in his life. But that said, it will be pure in the next life. In the next one, they will stay together and not ping pong back and forth through each other's lives. It's love. The thing making a mockery of most all of us. Ben and Heather have the sort of true eternal love that we all strive for. What, if I'm honest, I still haven't found. But with a touch of luck, Ben and Heather, Heather and Ben, well, they will keep pulsing back and forth and end together. Love.

SEIZURE

I'M BRUSHING MY TEETH when the seizure hits. My jaw clamps tight on bristles and plastic. My head nods down and then up again. The bathmat starts to slide. I bend my knees and grab the slick marble counter. My vision blinks out. This is the first one, but I know more will come.

My sister steps into the bathroom after it leaves me and I've drooled toothpaste all over my chin. Alice wears a white button down, pleated skirt, and saddle oxfords. Everyone tells me that she is the most beautiful girl in school. I try not to hear them.

"You are the most disgusting human being on the planet. Can I please have the bathroom now?" she asks.

"Get out, or I'll snap your bird neck." I say, and then feel guilty for saying it.

"Get out, or I'm telling Dad you said that," she says with sharp tones. "And I'm telling him where you hide your cigarettes."

"Tell him and you'll never get another." I say, letting the words fall like coins.

"I have my own, thank you very much." She slams the door.

I wipe my chin and check myself in the mirror. I look healthy. My eyes are clear and when I pull my skin it jumps back into place. I can't see anything wrong. I can't feel anything either, but somehow I know this isn't over. This isn't the first one, so I know more will come.

At school, Madison Kale breaks a pencil in half by lacing it through his fingers and smacking his hand down on the desk. Digger, we don't know his real name, asks if it hurts. His eyes are black dots behind thick glasses.

"Shut your hole!" Madison says. He turns to me, "Got any smokes?"

"Yeah," I say. "Let's ditch."

From Madison's roof, I can see Crescent Lake. I can see Alice sitting with her linebacker boyfriend on a park bench. And I can see our old Victorian house on the corner. The house Dad sold when I got sick. It's the house Mom left when she couldn't take us anymore. Madison fishes two cigarettes from the pack and lights one. He hands me the other. In the time it takes for Madison to do this, I catch myself from falling down. Digger doesn't smoke.

"There's this girl at school with a pig valve in her heart," he says.

"That works?" Digger asks.

"Guess so," he says. "I hear she swims on the team now."

"I should try that," I say and even think I mean it. "I could be a swimmer."

The wind kicks up and I crush my cigarette out on a black shingle. Madison climbs up on the chimney and lies down so that his chest lies on a concrete slab. He twirls his arms and kicks his legs. He turns his head to the side for air.

Digger says to please be careful. I'm thinking I'll try that too, swimming on the chimney. But my head nods down and then up again. My jaw clamps shut. I lose all balance and start to fall.

Digger lifts his hands up toward Madison with the hope he might catch him. He faces the other way. I wish he would turn around and see me beginning to fall.

OUR ROUTINE

IN A FOG OF WORRY, I attempt to start over. I've got my hands in the hands of a little guy, nine years old. The electric energy of youth eases my worry, but does not stop it. This is Pete. Pete's mom and I are on fast forward to love, and it worries me. Pete tells me to please, please, please let go of his hands and bait his hook. So I do. We stand at the end of a little dock in a little town at the bottom of Alabama on the bay. Jeb comes out in his usual fashion, places a bucket at his feet, tosses out a line and lights a cigarette at the same time –a trick of incredible manipulation. Jeb has a raspy voice usually heard in movies about pirates. Pete suddenly screams, "Got one!" and we both stop what we are doing and watch Pete's line.

Pete's mom, Angela, and I bring Pete to the pier to fish often. Pete always has fun, always catches more than we do, and always wants my 'secret' candy bar that I bring in my back pocket for him. Angela arrives after we have already set up and Pete is reeling in what looks to be a croaker. She had a doctor's appointment and the pale yellow lines of worry at her eyes remind me that her chronic Leukemia is a serious thing.

"Reel that lil' croaker in, buddy!" Jeb cries out to Pete. Jeb rubs out his cigarette, and tosses in the empty bucket brought for that reason. At times, he'll rinse it and bring a few fish home to his ailing wife, but mostly it is an easy target for cigarette butts.

Pete leans back and shoots the croaker over the pier railing, and onto the boards. Jeb has already put his reel down and scoops the croaker up and effortlessly removes the hook. He tosses the little fish at Pete, who in that instant, empties his hands and catches the fish.

While Pete eyeballs the croaker, I lean to Angela.

"What did the doc say?" I ask.

"As usual, cryptic nonsense and psychobabble about my need for a counselor."

"And your response?"

Angela exhales loudly and exclaims, "I'm all better, you son of a bitch!"

"What did you really say?" I watch Pete eyeball the fish.

"Mom, you aren't supposed to cuss."

"I know, sweetie... Forgive me?"

This is our routine, going on five years now.

I am trying to figure Angela out, and as all men do, I fail at understanding the finer points of fascination, lust, bewilderment, compassion, empathy, and plain love.

"So, Angela, can I help this time?"

"No, I am afraid that, as usual, the doctors want tests and tests take time and money. You just be you, and be good to Pete. That is all I ask."

"Oh, come on, there has to be something I can do?"

"Bait that man's hook!" Angela goes in behind Pete and takes up the rod and reel, pointing it at me. She rests her chin on Pete's shoulder and watches the croaker gasp. Pete steps forward and tosses him back.

"Good luck, little man, you swim fast now, you hear?"

"Good, little Pete, throwin' em back to fight another day."

"Sure, but if I get a bigger one, he's goin' home to fry." Pete starts laughing and Angela joins in. Her laugh is, without a doubt, the sexiest thing I have ever heard.

And the two of them giggle on like that until Pete does, in fact, hook a bigger croaker and they plan a meal.

"I want lemon on it!" Pete cries out. Jeb gives him a high five after the fish is on the pier. Jeb always high five's Pete after a fish is brought in. And Angela always fries his fish in a skillet with extra lemon. And we have a glass of wine, and clink glasses. And we smile at one another until Pete goes to bed. Then we meet again, suddenly just kids ourselves, and make love to light jazz, and attempt to enjoy our lives.

Just the same, Leukemia is rough. And I worry. And I often wonder how Angela does not worry more.

She says, "You are my safety net. If something happens to me, Pete has you." To which I nod and smile. My assurance that I am a part of her world is a deep, and lovely, thing.

And bringing Pete into my world has been an experience of pure joy. Frustration too, sure, but oh the joy of that look in a boy's eye when he has done something to please you, then realizes he has succeeded, and the smile that follows. Pete now, for example, looks to me having released the fish and smiles while saying, "Fight another day, buddy!" It almost brings tears to my eyes.

"Another one!" Pete screams, and as Jeb moves in closer, Debbie walks out to our end of the pier. Debbie claps and whistles and coughs out, "Fish on!" Debbie has given up smoking, but still sounds like she is the two-packs-a-day smoker she once was.

Debbie moves in, helping Pete keep the line from tangling on the railing, and eases the line to the far end of the pier where Pete can stand and reel, unhindered. Pete pulls up a croaker twice the size and holding the line, turns to Angela with hopeful eyes.

"Dinner?" Pete asks.

"Of course, Pete. That is a big man making us dinner!" Angela squeezes my arm and pulls me into a sort of sideways hug. I squeeze back.

"Great job, Pete! Threw the little guy back to go tell his grandpa to come back and see us!" I squeeze Angela and stop thinking about her illness for the longest 30 seconds of my life.

Jeb comes closer and all four of us circle Pete and the big ole croaker. We have become a circle of love. The Leukemia takes a back seat for the moment, and I am deeply moved. I high five Pete and help him with the hook and lower the reel to the boards. I high five Pete a second time, rare for me, but I exclaim, "Little big man just caught us dinner!"

Angela gives me a high five, also rare, and we look into each other's eyes and know our love is true. Sick or not, we love one another, we love Pete, and we will muscle our way through this, to the very end.

TIMES I NEARLY DIED

Non-Fiction

WHEN I WAS BORN with Hyaline Membrane Disease. The doctors gave me even odds. My father was out hunting, drunk.

When Scarlet Fever found me.

When the old dude who lived next door's tree house gave way to one hundred feet of tree limbs, hitting and falling, then hitting again. My torso tangled in the rope swing, dangling six feet above the hard, root-filled dirt.

When my father took me hunting, drunk, and shot a hole through the hood of our truck. When my father took me anywhere.

When my brother threw a brick at my head in ambush. His aim was very good.

When I learned to drive. When I learned to drink. When I learned to combine them.

When I introduced my girlfriend to my father. When my father met her mother. When my father married her mother. When that girl said, "Let's keep dating."

When I was jogging, then hit by a car, and my body flipped up onto the hood. My face pressed to the glass, inches from the driver's face. When the driver slammed on the brakes, catapulting me off the hood and into the street. I never found my radio.

When I learned my college dormitory would be coed. When I looked in the mirror, naked, and thought about what that meant.

When the redneck shot me with a blow-gun and all I could think of was poison. When my mother arrived at the hospital with her shirt on backwards and inside out. When we got home and a man I didn't know sat at the kitchen table, smoking cigarettes.

When my brother married and moved away. When he and his wife let me hold their first-born child.

When the boat ran in reverse, and no one knew it but me, waltzing with propeller blades in six feet of water.

When I free climbed a 100 foot pitch, in hiking boots, because I couldn't listen to that girl say one more word.

When I climbed the Grand Teton, and the rope wasn't long enough. I started up the pitch, not yet on belay, with 5,000 feet of exposure. When the guide finally made the top, clipped in, and turned around smiling. He laughed. My fingertips bled.

When I quit climbing.

When I quit that girl.

When I forgave my dying alcoholic father, and he looked at me and asked, "For what?" When, at the funeral, my father's best friend squinted and asked me, "Why couldn't you have been a team player?" and I smelled whiskey on his breath.

When I asked the new girl to marry me, guessing I had even odds.

When she said "Of course." Frantic, I asked, "Does that mean 'yes'?"

When she said, "Yes. That means 'yes'."

When we drank a few bottles of wine, after the marriage, and we discussed moving to Mobile.

When she said, "Well, we both have parents there." When I said, "and the ocean and the Bay is so close." I looked at our dog and asked, "What do you think, girl? Should we move?" When she, of course, said nothing.

In the morning, I wanted to take all our recycling to the center so there would be room for that evening's guests.

I made it exactly one half mile before I eased through a green light and a man on the right side of the intersection decided he could make it if he gunned it. So he made it up to 40mph before he hit me. When it was a solid hit, pushing me into the next lane and getting hit by an SUV, minding its own business.

The worst part is that I knew the people in the SUV and worse still was having known their eldest son, who killed himself. I thought about it for months afterwards, "Why them, and for God's sake, why me?"

They are the nicest people, and I never even remember hitting the brakes. In fact, I don't remember a solitary thing. Everything I know has been told to me. Sometimes, When I look at the pictures, someone with car-knowledge will be sure to say, "No way anyone survived that wreck!" I sheepishly raise my hand and tell them, "Well I did."

When then they say, "You are one lucky motherfucker."

I try to think of that statement When I'm either getting in or out of the wheelchair and not feeling very lucky.

So after that I was told the old high school was keeping my job secure for me. My wife had started her fundraising job for the school while I was recovering.

When I felt like a charity case.

When I went to therapy five days a week and tried to get myself better. When it was no use. When I decided I should try myself.

So I thought as an act of independence, I should clean myself up without help. I got my hands clean and was washing my face before I fell. I had gotten blurry vision in the wreck which was worsened by the soap getting in my eyes.

When I got dizzy and fell. I tried to stop my fall by grabbing a hand towel. It slowed me down but then my weight kicked in and the towel bar came flying out of the wall.

When I hit the floor, butt–first. When I realized I was okay and grabbed the side of the counter-top. When I pulled myself up to a standing position and grabbed the now fallen hand towel to wipe my face. When I realized how far back the wheelchair had become and knew I couldn't make it.

When I got myself back down on the floor and crawled to the wheelchair.

When I thought, as I was pulling myself up to the seat, "Why is my life like this?"

When I decided, "Back to therapy."

Then I thought about Shane. He had been my best friend. Shane, as usual, was out kayaking. It was a freak accident. He just wanted to shake the leaves out of his hair.

So Shane, like always, wiggled his hips and flipped the kayak over. So far, so good. Then When he had finished an underwater shake and tried to flip back to the surface, he realized that his kayak was stuck between a fallen tree and a rock.

When he couldn't get the rest of the turn done. He stared up at the surface and tried everything he could think of. But he was where he was and not able to get the kayak free, he finally couldn't stand it and took a breath.

What that really meant was sucking a large amount of water into his lungs. I'm sure that at that moment, he thought about his wife Alison and if she would be okay? Then he drowned.

When Alison told me the news.

When my brother told me that the name of his little girl, who was in my arms, was Allison. I smiled and looked up and said "All right Shane, she is fine. Don't need to worry about her."

Whenever I see Allison and she smiles and says, "Hi Uncle Murray, let's have some fun!"

When, on some days, it brings tears to my eyes.

When on most days, it makes me smile.

LAST WILL AND TESTAMENT

YOU DON'T KNOW THIS, but I did everything in my power to convince my father to change his cockamamie will. I'm a lawyer for Christ's sake.

It's hardly a reasonable document. Most of us will end up with nothing. Nothing! After all those weekends in a drafty cabin in godforsaken Barlo, supposedly hunting. Of all the cover stories, *hunting!* Eleanor made it all sound fairly legitimate, but Bennett only hunted when he worked himself into an angry drunk. And at that point it wasn't hunting. It was killing. Daddy would drink all day and then something insignificant, a dropped glass or broken ashtray, would send him into a rage. He'd grab his rifle and ride the four-wheeler down the swamp road with a high beam spotlight. He'd see a pair of eyes and fire that damn cannon of a rifle. What was it? A seven millimeter mauser. A cannon is what it was. I have tinnitus just from standing next to him. Sometimes he actually killed a buck, but most times not. Fawns, doe, wild boar, coyote; Bennett didn't care. The game warden was on the dole so he didn't care either. They'd call up some poor black guy from the squatter's camp and have him drag the kill —whatever it happened to be- back to the cabin, skin it out, and butcher the meat. They'd pay him off, send him on his way, and then celebrate the successful hunt with a bottle of whiskey.

"Hunting, my ass," I said.

"I did the best I could with what I had," Eleanor, an x-wife, said. "There wasn't much."

I was trying to tell the others about the will, but the mind wanders.

"Get on with it, Wallace." Ren pumped his fist. "For God's sake!"

Shane took off his shirt and wrapped it around his head like a sheik's headdress. He sat with crossed legs on the pinestraw and placed his hands, palm up, on his knees. He closed his eyes and took deep, even breaths. He's always been some kind of an alternative freak.

"This is church property, Shane," Celia, another x-wife, said to her son. "Put your shirt back on."

"You were a stripper," Shane said. "Beside, a little mediation might be just the thing for this place. Walrus here could use it. Ren too. Look at his face."

"This heat is oppressive," Eleanor said. "I'm going back to New Orleans. Even Katrina didn't stir up this much shit."

"But I put up with it," I continued. "I greased the wheels. I played the role of son. I bought an olive green goose feather jacket and acted like I gave a damn. I thought it would all pay off. I thought Bennett would recognize my loyalty and leave me a fair share of his wealth. His wealth. What a joke! He inherited every penny and spent more than he made. Which is pretty damn greedy when you think about how much money he had to begin with. How can you start with twelve and a half million dollars and end up with seven? How can anyone spend so much, make so little, and then leave everything to chance?"

Ren's face was as red as a party balloon. He pumped his fist, leveled his eyes, and growled, "Spit it out, Walrus."

I gave Ren my look that says *don't you dare call me that* but I knew I'd better move on. Even I was antsy to get this out.

"A game of craps!" I said. "That's his idea of a will. All seven million dollars will go to the wife or son who throws the best dice. I think Georgia gets a boat, but other than that, it's all or nothing. Winner take all."

"What about me," Celia said, her eyes suddenly clear and focused.

"What are craps?" Joy asked.

"You roll like the rest of us," Wallace said to Celia.

"And what boat? What does Georgia have to do with this?" Celia asked. The x-wives were unclear about who each other was, children included.

"Craps!" Shane shouted. "Excellent."

"I could kill him," Ren said, his jaw grinding.

"Too late," Shane said.

Baxter jogged in place, eyes darting from brother to brother.

"One game?" Ren asked. "One roll of the dice for seven million? There are two wives, five children, and seven million dollars. Why not an even split?"

"Is this bathroom humor?" Joy asked. "I've never gone in for bathroom humor."

"Didn't even consult me on the legalese of the document," I explained. "Went to some other lawyer up in Birmingham. Some Mr. Bridges so and so. And it's bullet proof. I can't find any way out of it. We meet tomorrow at the courthouse at noon."

"We'll sue the will," Celia said. "Can you sue a will? Did you say *five* children?"

"It's perfect," Shane said. "It's the treasury of desire."

"I think you're behind this, Walrus," Ren said. "I bet this is your doing. I'm bringing my own dice."

I gave him my look again, but what more can you do at your father's funeral?

"Good idea," Shane said. "If we all bring loaded dice, we'll all win."

"Shut it, Buddha boy," Ren shouted. "This is serious."

"Georgia is his daughter?" Celia asked. She opened her purse and took out a medicine bottle, tapping out two tablets and swallowing them without water.

"This is all too much," Eleanor said. "Call me when you come to town, Wallace."

"Mr. Bridges will have the table and dice at the courthouse. Bennett made the arrangements. We could contest it, but we'd all have to agree. And if we did, it could take forever. Plus, the judges in this town might not budge. They think shenanigans like this are hysterical.

Alabama. What in God's name am I doing here? I should be over in New Orleans playing the real game. I should use my considerable intellect for something other than these small town, southern shenanigans."

My brothers shouted and paced. Celia whined. Joy mumbled.

Then Baxter suddenly stopped running in place. He carefully slipped off his shoes and unbuckled his belt. Then he unzipped.

We all stopped what we were doing.

Baxter removed his pants. Underneath, he wore nylon running shorts. He put his running shoes back on, took off his button down shirt, and removed his undershirt. He stood before us bare-chested, zero-percent body fat, shaved head, and eyes full of tears.

"Honey," Celia said. "Are you okay?"

Baxter wiped his eyes and very calmly began to run.

The Porter family, if you can call it that, stood in silence as Baxter ran down the church driveway, past the fence, and onto the main road. I decided at that moment that if I won the dice game, I'd leave Alabama forever. Even if I didn't win, I had big plans brewing in New Orleans.

"Let him go." Shane said. "Running is his meditation."

We watched in silence until he was entirely out of sight. Then we started fighting again.

RUNNING MULE HOLLOW

THE ROADS IN MULE HOLLOW are long and wide, unfrequented by cars, and in summer months, make for the perfect place to run. The sides of the road are flat, and a beaten path threading through wild flowers give safe asylum from the occasional logging truck. Beyond the path, cabins and deer-filled valleys spread out like knit blankets, and beyond that, the sharp-crested mountains hold on greedily to the last patches of winter snow. The mountains are big enough that no matter how fast or how far you run, the view never changes. Even when I run a twenty mile loop, circumnavigating Mule Hollow entirely, the mountains stare down on me, unimpressed and unmoved.

The town itself is small, about twenty thousand people, and the center of town, which I never run through, is only a few blocks of simple stores, a gas station and obligatory car wash, a grocery and pizza parlor. Most of the town works for the logging company, the ski resort, or during some hard winters, some commute fifty miles south to San Pieta for employment. On the west side of town, there is an alternative living community called Blessed Fields. The members have given up all personal possessions and any desire for personal gain, all for the sake of harmonious communal living. In order to survive, Blessed Fields became self-sufficient. They grow their own food, stitch their own clothing, and run an herbal remedy shop in town. It is common knowledge that Blessed Fields members support the medicinal use of marijuana, and that they sell it covertly under the counter at their shop. No one in town cares enough to put up a fight and quite a few locals buy more than Ginseng when they visit. In fact, I would be hard pressed to think of any of our young inhabitants who didn't take advantage of the Blessed System, aside from me, as weed makes me nauseous.

Katie told me that when her father died, she had taken all of the photo's she could find of him and made a number of small collages. Then she had put each collage in a separate section of a wooden folding screen. This way, she said, she could look at her father in different lights, on different days, with different expressions, as if he were still around. Katie said that she had bought the screen with six places for photographs because that was as close as she could find to seven days a week, and thus, she could wake up and say hello to a new side of him every morning. When I asked about the seventh day, she said that on Sundays we slept late with hangovers, and she would rather not see him like that anyway.

I usually run in the late afternoons. I'm stiff and groggy with thick legs in the morning, and I've sworn off the noon-day sun, so when I finish work at 4:30 or 5:00, -as a sculptor, this varies daily- I lace up my Asics and stretch my legs across the long country roads of Mule Hollow. I try to run different routes day to day; from the sandy shouldered east side roads along the graveyard, to the pine and patchouli-scented gravel west of town. Some days I run for six miles, some days ten, and some days twenty. I never know, or care, how far or how long I'm going to run. I don't wear a watch and I don't drive my route. Instead, I double knot my shoes, sunscreen my nose, and often carry music. But I do not enter races and I never keep track of time. Running is the only place where I am free from stress and pressure and from all the noise in my head.

Katie also tells me that while she misses her father badly, that there is a certain purity in the way things are now. She knows that he is not suffering, that he is free of need, and she knows that they will never fight again. She tells me that she talked with her father before he died and they had put all of their differences aside, which I guess means that they had put me aside, but I don't say that. She also says that she wishes

I could do the same with my father. Katie pulls her soft, mocha hair back and tells me she is ok with her father's death. But I know Katie is a runner too. So when I see her coming up strong on the opposite side of the road with her brow crunched up and her hair black with sweat, and notice that she isn't wearing a watch either, I know that exercise is the furthest thing from her mind.

I have epiphanies when I run. Seriously. Sometimes I have small, unimportant epiphanies, like when I realized that the expression *for all intents and purposes*, was not, in fact, *for all intensive purposes* as I had thought for most of my life. But there are times when I have the real thing. Life changing realizations that come to me in an anaerobic flash. Once during a fifteen miler, I stopped running entirely, put my hand to my head, and coughed and wheezed as I realized my father had cheated on my mother with my 3rd grade baby-sitter. It wasn't that I had come across any new evidence; I had not spoken to anyone new or found anything, it was just that I had looked closely at a ten year old's memory with a thirty year old mind. Then there was the time that I realized my then-girlfriend was bulimic. The odd amount of time spent in the bathroom, the constant talk of caloric intake, fat grams, and metabolic process… Running along the Blessed Fields vegetable garden, it hit me like an aneurysm.

And so I run Mule Hollow. In a clouded daze of memories and realizations. Like we all have –I suppose, but mine occur on the run. And it turns out, I run around Mule Hollow, keeping the town just inside my path, but tussling the mountains to the outer edge. And it may seem senseless, but I am most at peace when I am out of oxygen and circling our tiny mountain town in a forward lean. It is that hour or two that I sort through the logistics of sculptures I am working on, or invent new ones. And in that same time, I recommit myself to art. The art of art. And my movements to stay clear of any 9 – 5.

And that brings us to the real story I hope to tell you here. That of Mule Hollow, the town I call home, and that of Katie, who's love I crave with a cocaine-like addiction. Katie teaches at the only elementary school in the Hollow, and that includes the gifted children. Once, Katie explained to me that smart kids are smart, but gifted kids have a way of thinking that is just plain different. Katie was a gifted child and her insights here amaze me.

As for my father, he died last summer. Katie begs me to make amends, even now. She says to write a letter, drive it to his grave, leave it with the birds. She says the mental act of writing followed by the physical trouble of the road-trip and the psychological symbolism of leaving it at his grave will do enough. So I have packed our hybrid and am ready. I've asked Katie to join me, and she has agreed on the condition that we not make it a vacation of any sort.

So we pack up, and are off. The drive to Montrose isn't bad. Just a long straight shot. Ten hours long. And why we can't fly is not clear, except that Katie says I have to endure a struggle. And struggle, I do. In mid-build of a sculpture that seems Calder-like, and almost whimsical, I force myself to freeze the genesis of it and strive to make Katie happy. Like I said, Katie's love is my cocaine, and most all of my movements circumscribe to her happiness. I remind myself of this after five hours driving on the road in a hybrid car that only seems happy at 60 miles an hour. Now, entirely worth it for the MPG's, but plain silly on the highway. Maybe I just got a lemon?

As the highway scrolls by, we discuss an incident at school.

"You know, I had a gifted child yesterday who has William's Syndrome , you know, I told you she is not able to distrust... Anyway, she told me that the clean-up man asked to see if she would lift up her shirt. So she did of course, but can you imagine? An eight year old with no breasts whatsoever, and this jerk does that? I can't get over this and where it could have gone."

"Holy smokes," I say. "Really?"

"Really. I told our principal and she fired him. No discussion."

"Good."

"I hope this child learns." Katie says as she leans back to stretch.

"Me too. It has to be the strangest way to grow up." I drive on in sincere disbelief.

"The odd thing is, there is really nothing anyone can do."

"Crazy."

"So you and your father," Katie begins. "I'm thinking you can let go after you leave him that letter."

"I pray," I say as I pat my chest pocket where the letter sits.

"Just be sure to acknowledge what you are doing as true communication with him."

"I'll try. But I'm not sure I know how to speak to the dead."

"Just know that he knows. That is all." Katie stretches and looks out her window as the Bay comes into sight.

"We must be close," Katie yawns out.

"Yes, just ten more minutes."

We do reach Montrose after a painfully long conversation about how my father still holds power over me, if I let him. Ten minutes never took so long. But we coast in and I show Katie the main drag, and where my Dad lived growing up. Then we stop at Wintzell's Oyster House for a bite before going to the graveyard.

"Fried oysters, huh?" Katie seems confused.

"See the sign? 'Fried, Stewed, or Nude...'" I point to a drawing my high school science teacher made on the wall.

"Ugh." Katie hasn't learned to love the South. "So so, Ben. This place gives me the creeps."

"Creeps or not, the food is terrific!" I state with confidence. Although, I wish Katie had ordered seafood, not the spaghetti. I didn't even know they had that here.

We finish, and as it turns out, the spaghetti was great. As always, my oysters were excellent, and I am very relieved that our start to the graveyard trip will begin right. With full bellies and tired eyes, we plod on to the graveyard. Now fully night.

"Can't we wait until morning?" I ask.

"No, it will be better that you have struggled through the entire day. This makes it work better. You have to believe that you have earned this."

"Hmmm. A ten hour drive, an odd conversation about a pervert, a great meal, and this is supposed to help?" I scratch my head conspicuously.

"None of those specifics matter. It is that you struggled to get here. And that you can leave your father in peace. You will sleep well tonight."

"I hope you are right, my dear. But if those oysters give me gas, you won't." I smile wide.

"Oysters or none, you'll sleep hard." Katie squeezes my hand. "Come on, Ben."

We make the graveyard in moonlight. I take the letter from my chest pocket. We walk in silence to my father's grave. I open the letter, unfold the sheet of paper, and lie it on top of the tombstone. A gust of wind catches it, and the letter floats over to the next grave, Crawford Filbone.

"Crawford here might not like what I have to say."

"Hmmm. Just lie it on the soil of your father's, don't balance it on top of the tombstone."

"OK." I unfold the paper again, and lay it on the soil. I use a stone to hold it in place. "How is this?"

"Perfect. Now say whatever is on your mind to him. I'll be over by the car." Katie walks slowly away.

"So Dad. Hiya there. Comfy? I don't know what in the hell I'm doing, but if it makes Katie there happy, I'll do it." I look to Katie now at car-side and smile. "You have to let go of me, Dad. At least, I'm hoping that's what you'll do. It's been a year now. I miss you, Dad. I miss your laugh. I miss having those dinners." I look over the grave searching for something to talk about. "This is horseshit, Dad. Absolute horseshit." I cross my arms and hope for a breeze. "OK buddy. Hope that did the trick. Or at least convince, Katie."

I uncross my arms and walk to the car.

"How did it feel?" Katie asks.

I consider my answer and the night ahead, "Peaceful. It was very peaceful."

"Oh, good," Katie says. "I'm so happy to hear you say that."

"I felt closure." I say. "Closure."

"Well, hmmm, I'm not sure it works like that. But if you feel good, I'm happy."

"I thought closure is what we were after?" I ask.

"Well, closure would be something you felt in a few days or weeks, or months or years… Not right now. You are not fifty feet from his grave. You have to let this happen. You can't force it."

"Oh. Ok. Then I feel however a guy should feel fifty feet from his father's grave."

"You are not taking this seriously, Ben." Katie folds her arms and sighs.

I raise my eyebrows, "What do you want to see?"

"I want you to FEEL this. No eyebrow raising allowed." Katie replies.

"I'm full and tired and would like to find a hotel to lie down," I say.

"I hope you've seen enough to heal, Ben." Katie says.

"Point anywhere, and I will stare. I don't know what I am supposed to do?"

"OK, to the hotel." Katie raises her palms and turns to face the car.

We sleep fitfully and rise early, returning to the highway. We talk little. Mid-afternoon, and we are already crossing into Mule Hollow.

"Learn anything?" Katie asks as I pull into our driveway.

"I learned not to be honest when you try to mess with my head. I learned to be as vague as possible so that we can remain at peace. I learned a ten hour car ride is miserable in our hybrid."

"Really? That's all you can say?" Katie asks without waiting for an answer. She goes inside and shuts the door.

I unpack, stretch, and put on Asics. I'm out the door and running just as the sun dips beneath the mountains. Katie has done the same. We leave headed in opposite directions, which means we will cross paths in about six miles. As predicted, after six miles, I see Katie's mocha ponytail and furrowed brow. Per her usual, she has no watch, and is so deep in this hypnotic ritual, barely realizes who I am.

"Katie, stop for a second. I'm sorry about how things went. I just wasn't sure what I was supposed to do or how to feel."

"I know, Ben, I guess I just hoped it might come to you. I'm not really sure what I expected either." Katie bends down to stretch her hamstrings.

I chuckle and it hits me. "You know, Katie… You know what I have realized? I have the same laugh as my father. And I miss his laugh, but I guess if I have his laugh, then I act as the second coming of him. Or something like that."

"Woah, Ben." Katie stands straight and smiles. "It has worked! You get it! My god, am I happy to hear you say this!"

"Really? Because we have the same laugh?" I silently realize that the whimsy of my new sculpture will benefit from all of this, after all.

"No, not that. It is that you realize you miss the man who made you, and know where you come from! I'm VERY happy we went! At last!" Katie gives me a high five that I am not sure how to react to. But, in the end, Katie is happy, and that is all that matters. And as a bonus, I have sudden motivation to finish new work.

We turn and begin our jog home, but this time, we run side by side. I ask Katie if she expects the scene at school tomorrow to revolve around the incident. She says "yes," and looks over to me.

"He was fired and that ends it," Katie reties her ponytail. "But I know everyone will have gossip."

"I'm just glad no one was hurt," I say.

"The thing is, I saw the whole thing. I turned him in. If I had not of seen it, he would not be fired. And I know he hates me for it. I'm nervous he'll come back for revenge."

"Shit. I didn't think of that. Maybe you should stay home for a few days. Let this all blow over?" I scratch my head.

"No," Katie replies. "I need to go back and stand my ground. I know the principal will call in more security. There will always be people around."

"Good. I don't want you alone."

"Me either. But I know I won't be. And now that you are at peace, I can see you'll be home sculpting in vigor."

"Yes, thank you for giving this to me." I lengthen my stride and Katie stays with me, chugging our route as the sunlight flits about the mountain line.

"No, you gave it to yourself. I just had to nudge you in the right direction."

"Thank you just the same," I say.

"Ok, catch me if you can." With that Katie speeds up into a near sprint and leaves me wondering if I can, in fact, catch her. Running full speed, I stare at Katie and grin, letting my father's laugh come right out.

"I got her, Dad," I say. "I got her."

BUDDY

AFTER BUYING THE HOUSE, Ben and Devon moved in, got settled, and found themselves talking about kids. They sat on the back porch, looked over the new expanse of trees, and discussed hanging a swing.

"We always had a swing when I was a kid," Ben said. "No matter how often Dad's job moved us."

"Us too," Devon replied. "We didn't move that much, so it became a staple of my time, outside the confines of the walls."

"Kids," Devon said.

"Are we ready?" Ben looked at Devon with concern.

"Is anyone?"

"I know, but really, shouldn't we get settled into our jobs first, at least?"

"Only to have me on maternity leave?"

"Yeah. I know." Ben scratched behind his head.

"We could get a dog first?" Devon smiled wide. "You know, break us in?"

Ben returned a smile and said, "You may be on to something, love. We have to build a fence. The deer won't appreciate a new beast roaming free. Or our neighbors."

"And what would we name it?" Devon scratched the back of her hand.

"Hmmm. I had a great dog once named Zuppa. After Zuppa Inglase, the Italian dessert."

"Zuppa?" Devon raised her eyebrows.

"Yeah. Zuppa. It's unique, and easy to say." Ben was very satisfied with his idea, but Devon wasn't convinced.

"But is that bad luck? Zuppa isn't with you anymore."

"You are right? We need a buddy, so how about Buddy?"

"Buddy." Devon said it again. "Buddy." Now she seemed okay with it.

"Buddy it is!" Ben called out. "A fence, then Buddy!"

"Oh boy, a fence." Devon shrugged. "I hate to do that to our patch of woods, but I know you are right. A dog needs a fence. This ought to create a puzzle for us to solve. Who, when, and where..."

"Honey, I see where you are going with this, but it'll be no trouble. I'll handle it. You just relax." Ben arched his back and put his hands behind his head.

"Well, shit, Ben, I can see it already. This has massive disaster written all over it."

In the morning, before work, Ben made a call to a friend.

"Adam, so what do you know about fences?"

"Keep stuff out, and keep stuff in," Adam replied.

"But building them..." Ben let his voice fade out.

"You need me. I can build you a fence. But. That said, you need to decide what you keep out, and what you keep in. That's all you."

"Yeah. I have the realtor coming by to show me the property lines, then we need something for a dog. Dog's need a fence."

"So do some people," Adam added.

"Well, you deal with the people. We just need one for a dog. We hope to get one soon. Very."

"What'll you name the little fella?"

"Buddy, as we need a buddy..."

"Buddy? Really? Seems like it might to too obvious. Odd choice." Adam crossed his arms and looked confused.

"We need a buddy."

"OK, a buddy it is. Buddy."

"Buddy."

"Yeah, I admit it has a ring. Just too obvious."

"Who cares?" Ben began to get annoyed.

"Your neighbors will want to know why you are calling out 'Buddy' to no one. And you'll want to check with them about those property lines. Has to be right."

"You bet Adam. Rose'll come in the morning tomorrow."

***

AND ROSE ARRIVED FIRST THING, as promised. She walked the property line with Ben, until they came to a neighbor, standing in the wooded shade.

"Hi, Neighbor. Ben." Ben produced an extended hand.

"Brent. Nice too meet you." Brent said. "You know I had some trouble with the guy who lived in your place last time. I hope we don't have that trouble."

"Well, I guess that depends on what the trouble was over?"

Brent stood in Birkenstocks, smoked, and had hair pulled back into a ponytail. He was a retired minor rock star.

"Property line. This is you starting at this oak, but the land east of it is mine."

"Huh. I figured it would go a bit closer to your place. Right Rose?"

Rose was measuring with her finger in the air. Rose stopped and began to write on a clipboard. She crossed and crisscrossed. Then she looked up at Brent.

"Brent, I'm afraid I have to tell you the line falls about ten steps beyond that oak. To the Laurel."

"Where are you getting this information?" Brent began to pace. His ponytail swished back and forth across his shoulders.

"These are the property lines my real estate agency has marked. For years, we have used these lines." Rose stared at her papers.

"Ok, ok, ok," Ben said. "Let's split the difference. I'll build a fence at that pine halfway between…" Ben smiled at his conclusion.

"Nope," Brent said. "I say the oak is the line. And thus our little problem with the last owners."

"Really?" Ben asked. "You can't accept the pine as meeting me halfway?" Ben began to feel anger.

"The oak," Brent said. "The oak. And I'll call my buddy at the state to prove it."

"Hey, hey, hey…." Ben stammered. "Slow down there pal. No need to make trouble. But if you have a guy at the state office who knows, I'd love to hear what he has to say."

***

AND SO THEY CALLED THE STATE OFFICE and had a man sent out. He walked the property with his map, and was obviously on Brent's side, as they seemed to be old friends.

"Nope, Brent, hate to say it, but this guy is right. The Laurel tree. Or whatever that is." Jimbo leaned into the Laurel and grabbed it for balance. "This."

"That is a Bay Laurel. People cook with the leaves. But it was here when we bought this place, and I am not a good cook." Ben stood straight backed. "Look, Brent, I'll still split it with you. The pine works for me."

"Yeah, you've got me beat. I'll take the pine. Thanks. I wrote a song back in the day about meeting halfway… I always liked that tune, so yeah, halfway works. The name of the song was 'Fences" and paid for my house, so I better do just that." Brent began to hum, moving into a pace of sorts that left Ben wondering if he really was ok. But ultimately, Brent was okay with the property line, and it was clear where the fence would be built.

***

AND SO THE DIFFERENCE WAS SPLIT, the fence was put in place, and Ben and Devon went to the Humane Society to adopt a dog.

They looked each one up and down, and discussed behavior issues that might arise.

"This guy sure is cute," Ben said. "But he has a touch too much energy. I'm afraid he would run us ragged." He held up the roar of spinning legs.

"And this little lady is scared of her own shadow. Not sure how well that would hold up in our woods?" Devon appeared exhausted.

"Alright…" Ben was calm. "Who have we got next?" He motioned for the adoption worker to bring another.

"Try this guy," the employee said. Then she placed a motley brown mop of fur in Ben's lap. "This one is new. I haven't even heard if anyone knows what kind it is?"

"The more mixed, the better." Ben was firm on this point. "Having grown up with pure-breds, I believe the more genetics the pup has to choose from, the better. Purebreds strike me as inbred."

"Well this guy seems to have what it takes," Devon smiled wide at the mutt before her. "Are you a little Buddy, buddy? Oh, I think you like the name Buddy!" The mutt wagged his tail hard and placed both front paws on Devon's arms, then inched forward and gave Devon a lick on her face.

"Well how about that. A little Buddy has found us after all, didn't ya buddy?" Ben squatted down and began to scratch the mutt on the back who was clearly now Buddy.

"Woopee!" Devon cried out at Buddy. "We've got ourselves a pup named Buddy!"

"You got that right," Ben said through his smile. "Maybe not my son, but damn close."

***

AT HOME, BUDDY INVESTIGATED the new fence and all of the land between that and the house. At close investigation, both Ben and Devon agreed that Buddy was a mix of Lab, border-collie, and maybe a hound. Buddy was a bit strange looking at first glance, but boy did he have a good heart. Tan with white spots and the ability to raise his eyebrows like no other dog they had ever seen. And black rings around his tail. He was a sight.

Brent walked to the fence and leaned over the top and looked down on Buddy. Buddy growled.

"Looks like you got a dog," Brent said. "I don't know what kind, but a four legged furball, for damn sure."

"Yes we do, Brent. Meet Buddy. And Buddy, no growling," Ben said this last part halfheartedly, and was a bit happy to hear Buddy growl.

"What is this thing?" Brent asked, lighting a joint but pretending it was a cigarette. Ben noted that it was clearly a joint.

"No idea," Ben said. "Full mutt. Good heart."

"Hmmm," Brent leaned over to pet Buddy, but Buddy would not stand close enough. "This thing have his shots?"

"Buddy has a full dose of vet-fix-it-shots," Devon replied.

"Buddy is entirely vaccinated if that is what you mean," Ben added. "And has enough love to give that he is curing us too."

"I suppose that kids are around the corner?" Brent asked.

"Slow down there," Devon said. "Probably, but for now, Buddy is all we need."

***

AFTER BEN WORKED WITH BUDDY, he would at last sit, shake, and stay. The three 'must do's that Ben insisted on. Devon wasn't sure why a dog really needed to 'shake,' but oh how Zuppa would do that one. 'Stay' was his weak point and any distraction took him off-base.

"Come on, Ben," Devon pleaded. "Let it go. If Buddy doesn't want to stay, so what?"

"Yeah," Ben replied. "I know. But it is such a simple thing. And what if our kids won't do that?"

"Buddy is a dog, Ben. The concept is more easily understood by us humans." Devon folded her arms.

"Right. I know. But I still think dogs understand an awful lot." To which Ben kneeled and shook Buddy's paw. "See?"

"Yeah. Buddy is your pal. I'd love to see that with a child."

"Me too… For now, this is good." Ben scratched Buddy's belly.

***

BEN AND DEVON AND BUDDY spent every evening on the back porch now that Buddy was held in by a fence. Buddy even learned how to fetch a tennis ball when either of them tossed it off the porch and into the yard. Both fed Buddy and both trained him, which gave everyone balance and kept things even. When suddenly, things changed.

"I'm pregnant," Devon said. "I'm at three weeks. But, I've heard to wait until 10 weeks before you tell anyone."

"I have to tell my Mom!"

"No, really. We should wait until it is safe. You don't want to have to tell your mother if I lose the child."

"Shit. Lose it? I hadn't thought about that. You're right."

"Can you keep this secret, Ben?"

"I'll try my best." Ben leaned in and took her hand, but Devon wasn't convinced. She gave Buddy a scratch and whispered in his ear, "Don't tell, Buddy. You can't tell no one, but you may have a little brother or sister on the way." Buddy wagged his tail, thumping the deck. Devon leaned back and smiled. Ben smiled too.

"So Buddy, you trust. Me… not so much."

"Yep," Devon looked Ben right in the eye and continued to smile.

***

AND AS LUCK WOULD HAVE IT, Devon went into labor months early, and then after a day in the ER, the baby could not hold on, and lose the baby she did. It was an angry moment that no one wished to relive, a sadness too great for words. Ben did his best to cheer Devon up, but all Devon seemed to want is to lie next to Buddy and hold him for an eternity. For Devon, it was a different world.

"You got Buddy with you, huh?" Ben stammered out of lack of anything better to say.

"Yeah Ben, Buddy and I get this sadness." Devon curled her body around Buddy and allowed him to lick her arms. Tears filled her eyes.

"Buddy, you take care of that momma of yours. You be her pal." Ben said in their direction. He then sat on the porch bench and tried not to cry.

"Come on Ben, let's just try again, don't you think? And move forward." Devon saw his eyes well.

"I think Buddy likes our current arrangement. And the fence that holds him now."

"Are you calling me a fence baby?" Devon raised her eyebrows, but also smiled.

"Why, yes, baby. You hold us together." Ben let a tear drop from his eye.

"And where does that leave me?" Devon asked. "I'm not sure I want to be in charge of you two." Devon cautiously smiled.

"Oh, just you be you. Buddy and I know where the property lines are. We can figure this out." Ben leaned back and exhaled.

"Fine by me. Just know that I'm not your boss. Maybe Buddy's, but not yours." With her arm around him, Devon gave Buddy a scratch on his chest.

"We'll try again one day. But for now, Buddy and I have you, our fence holding us together, and that is all we need." Ben tried to sound bright and cheerful.

"Ok, baby. I'll do my best, but just know I am not chain link." Devon forced a smile.

"I'd say you are old pine. Big planks of big ole pine holding us together. Holding us in."

NEIGHBORS

THE APARTMENT DOOR CLICKING shut wakes me. Charlotte walks in, smoking. She drops her cigarette into a beer bottle on the nightstand and lifts her gray sweater up and over her head. Feeling safe in the darkness, she unhooks her bra, exposing small, well-shaped breasts, eggshell white within the triangles of a bathing suit tan. I watch her surreptitiously, my eyes fully adjusted to the night. Charlotte pulls one of my t-shirts from the dresser, struggling to find the appropriate holes. She kicks off leather boots and stomps out of her jeans. The trademark logo of Havana 59, the restaurant where Charlotte works, is stitched into her panties. She crawls into bed as if her bones are made of rubber. I smell tequila, smoke, perfume, and sex when she presses against me, spooning beneath linen sheets.

"Have fun?"

"I guess. We drank too, too much."

"I can tell."

"What'd you do?"

"Worked till eight. Drank a beer at The Garage. Ran into Shane."

"How is he?"

"Bearded."

"Wintertime."

"Yeah."

Charlotte clutches at my waist, and I can tell she is spinning. She buries her face between my shoulder blades. The smell of her makes me sick, but I don't say it. I reach back and make sure she is covered. The alarm clock reads 4:52.

"Shit. My pill."

Charlotte gets up, becomes dizzy, and claws at the bed for balance. After a second of close-eyed concentration, she goes to her knees and digs through her purse in the dark. I hear jingles, clicks, and finally, "Got it." She swallows the pill without water and fumbles her way back to bed.

"I wish you had told me you would be so late."

"Why?"

"I worry about you."

"Worry, worry."

"Seriously."

"You're not my boyfriend."

"I know, but when you drink sometimes, you…"

"What's all this?"

Charlotte turns so that we lie back to back. Her toes press into my calf, and I can't believe how cold they are.

"Nothing."

I sleep fitfully, waking often and my throat becoming sore. I click off the alarm before it erupts, slip out of the bed, and tiptoe to the shower. I work Saturdays and let Charlotte sleep. I dress in the darkness, feeling for my boots and easing out into the den. I leave a note on the coffee table, Dinner tonight? Stop by at seven. —Ben. But I know that when I get off work, she will be gone. Out with other friends, other men, drinking and standing close. Charlotte lives next door, and the proximity is wearing me thin.

***

I STOP BY CHARLOTTE'S to see what she has planned for the weekend. Her roommate, Amy, answers the door.

"Where's Charlotte?"

"Gone, gone, gone, Ben." Amy twirls and sips root beer from the can.

"What? Where?"

"She drove over to Wintergreen and met up with some guy named Charles. She says he's a dentist. I bet he makes good money. I'd like to meet a dentist."

"Yes. Well, I…"

"Want to go down to Havana 59 and get a drink? Charlotte says that margaritas are half price right now. We should go get a drink. Don't you need a drink? Come on, Ben. Let's go!"

Amy twirls again and snatches up her fleece jacket. Behind her, leafless tree branches hold still beyond the window. Frost collects in the corners of the glass panes. Amy purses her lips and blots a napkin against them. She smiles, crimson red, and latches on to the crook of my arm.

The bar at Havana 59 is crowded with rich 20somethings and rich 50somethings. It is a brief period of time when parent and child can occupy the same space without collision. They glow with artificial tans and beaming white teeth. I check myself in the bar mirror but wish I hadn't. Amy, however, smiles and twirls and squeezes my hand.

"Margarita time! I want mine frozen, lime, and make sure they put it in one of those funny glasses that look like a goldfish bowl. And a straw. Don't look at me that way, this is fun." Amy twirls away.

I order without getting into specific types of glasses. A dark, plaintive-eyed girl taps my shoulder, offering up a tray of cigars, but I pass. The girl moves down the bar with manufactured enthusiasm, and I suddenly regret my decision. It is as though I have hurt her in some unseen way. Neon blinks on the girl's face through hazy cigar and cigarette smoke. A white-haired fat man buys a cigar and slips the girl a twenty. She tucks the bill into her hip pocket and smiles.

Amy catches up with old friends at an adjacent table. She tugs at her blonde hair and taps a suede cowboy boot. The couple at the table looks up to Amy's face with eyes wide. They grin and laugh and lean forward as she talks. The bartender brings my drink, scotch, and Amy's fluorescent green fishbowl. I am at once embarrassed by the bowl and relieved that the right one came. Amy returns and we drink and talk, our conversation passing from pleasant to sexual as the alcohol works our blood. In a show of bravado, or possibly fear of exclusion, we both purchase Cuban cigars and step outside. The cobbled terrace shimmers in lamplight, the Virginia night is cold, and Amy's hand slips into mine.

Back at my apartment, we tear at one another, clothes coming off and hitting the floor. I pull back the sheets and we're in, grappling and gripping and gasping for air. Our sex is electricity and heat. Ice groans and cracks at the windowpanes. I can't help myself, and I imagine she is Charlotte, pressing against me. I slide my fingers over her breasts. Cup my hands to the small of her back. I flex my hips. I kiss her mouth, her elegant neck. I reach for her hands and squeeze.

Charlotte and I have never done any of this. We drink together, eat together, and for a month now, sleep together, but nothing more. At once I realize I have fallen in love with her. And I'm fucking her roommate like a dog in heat. I open my eyes and look at Amy, flushed and beautiful. I run for the bathroom.

Charlotte returns on Sunday, and I know Amy tells her everything. I just know. Charlotte and Amy live in 3f, and I live in 3g. Our doors face one another, squared off like gunfighters. The floor plans are a mirror image. I turned my second bedroom into an office. A roommate would save money, but living with guys makes me nervous. I'd live with Charlotte if I could. For nearly a week I come and go at times I think I can avoid them both, staying at work as much as I can. I work for Richmond's outdoor outfitter, Blue Mountain. Tents, backpacks, boots, and everything else conceived to make a trip into the unknown comfortable.

***

AT THE STORE, Shane lances price tags through double-stitched, chemically treated shirts. I fold. Shane checks his watch.

"You're still here."

"So."

"Are you fucking Charlotte yet?"

"What? No. Not exactly."

"You don't want to go home, do you?"

"I'm broke, I need the hours."

"Bullshit."

Shane catches his thumb on the tagging gun, and an orb of cherry red blood swells between flesh and nail. He presses a paper towel down on it hard.

"What makes you think I want to fuck Charlotte?"

"Who wouldn't want to fuck Charlotte? Charlotte's good stuff. And didn't you say she was sleeping with you? But 'not sleeping with you,' whatever that means. What the hell are you up to out there?"

"Sure, she sleeps at my place sometimes. Doesn't like sleeping alone.But nothing else. We haven't even kissed."

"What the hell is that?"

"Look, it's good. It's a best friend I can lean on without feeling like a faggot."

"Hmm. And now you don't want to go home."

"Whatever."

"You fucked Amy." Shane grabs a handful of red beard and grins.

"No."

"Yes. You fucked Amy."

"Maybe."

"Damn, what was that like? I bet that girl twirls in bed. Good stuff, that twirling. But neighbors. Shit."

"Might be a problem."

"Never fuck a neighbor. That's the rule. You can't escape."

"Gee, thanks. Go tape your thumb."

***

IT'S LATE, but Charlotte and Amy's door is open. They leave it that way when they want me to stop over for a drink. I have about six more steps to decide what I should do. Charlotte pokes her head out with three steps left.

"I thought I heard you."

"Yeah."

"Where have you been all week? I've got the dirt on you." Charlotte points a finger at my chest and cocks her eyebrow.

"Work. Oh."

"Come in, Amy's out."

I step into the apartment and take a seat in a wicker chair near the door. Charlotte brings me a beer. She is wearing her hair down and casual. Her jeans look new— the way she fits in them, more sensual, more perfect— and her white silk shirt floats over her breasts, giving me the illusion of visibility. I quickly look down at my beer.

"So…"

"What, it was stupid. I'm sorry."

"Sorry? What are you talking about?"

"Well, she's fun. I mean, sure, I like her. How was your dentist?"

"Charles is my cousin."

"Cousin."

"He's great. We drove over to Wintergreen and went skiing Saturday. Had a blast. I called in sick Monday so we could catch a few more runs. You should have seen me on the blacks. I skied better than when we went." Charlotte scratches the back of her hand with pink fingernails. "I think I finally learned how to relax. Loosen up a bit."

"Really. So he's your cousin. That sounds like fun."

"You're acting funny."

"No I'm not."

"O.k."

"I've just been working too much this week. Inventory."

"Oh. Well. Are you going to ask Amy out for this weekend?"

"I don't know."

"Shit."

"What?"

"Don't do this."

I drink my beer and stare at the television while Charlotte lights a cigarette. Clint Eastwood is cutting a guy down with his Colt. He tells the guy how stupid he is after the guy is dead.

"What are you doing this weekend? Out of town again?"

"No. I thought I'd stick around here. Watch an apartment fling unfold."

"We could get dinner."

"With Amy?"

"With you."

"I think you better do that with Amy."

"Well."

"Well?"

"Yeah."

Charlotte steps to the window and presses her hand against the glass. Ravens caw. She pulls her hand away and shakes out the cold.

"I'm wiped out. I think I'm gonna go crash. You coming?"

"I think you better do that with Amy, too."

"Yeah. Well."

"Yeah."

"Goodnight Charlotte."

I stand up and take a step toward Charlotte, but she is already making for the kitchen with the empty beers. I let her go, and walk back into the hall. I stop for a moment between our apartments. With both doors shut, I can almost touch them at the same time. I'm an inch shy. The light in the ceiling buzzes, and I look at the collected moths, trapped and filling up the glass dome. I smell snow as a draft sweeps through the stairwell door. For now, I am content to stand here, in between apartments, neither tenant nor neighbor. It is late, the light flickers, and I swear I can hear the city groan.

FEIGNING NONCHALANCE

Non Fiction

"BISHOP SLOAN, due to car a car accident, I have a traumatic brain injury and amnesia. Thus, I write this letter to be sure I tell you everything without forgetting."

Feigning nonchalance, I continued, "I was married to my high school sweetheart when the wreck occurred. Her younger brother had died of cancer just six months before. She was unable to handle that loss in addition to my brain injury and confusion. For her, it was as if her husband had died in the wreck. Needless to say, I was more than a little confused. So, having passed driver's rehabilitation, I moved back to Athens, Ga., where I had lived with my first wife. I found myself away from friends and family, and lonely, so I tried on-line dating. It should not be a legal option for people with a brain injury to do this."

My knuckles turned white, "I had been awarded some money in the lawsuit following my wreck, and therefore, I was a target. I suffered through an ordeal I will not go into."

I sighed and continued, "By the grace of God, I was able to get out of that misery. I have also been blessed to be given the chance to start over in so very many ways."

"I was in a coma and then wheelchair at first," I added. "But not anymore."

Bishop Sloan eyed me fiddling with my pocket, but said nothing. The bishop is a big man, and an imposing presence, but after less than thirty seconds, Sloan puts you right at ease.

I continued, "My sister-in-law introduced me to Mary Balfour, and though we struggled initially with my short term memory loss, we have moved into a wonderful relationship. Mary Balfour understands my brain injury, and the things I still struggle with. For example, driving gives me anxiety, but I will move to be closer to Mary Balfour. This should also help Mary Balfour stay in her desired diocese. I just put down a deposit holding an apartment in Cahaba Heights Village. I have also been in touch with a man named Malcolm." I paused, looked up and added, "Mary Balfour introduced us…" Then I finished, "and plan to volunteer at Spain Rehabilitation once I get settled. I was airlifted to Spain following my wreck."

I could no longer stand it and removed a box from my pocket.

I finished, "Thank you, Bishop Sloan, for listening to all of this and understanding that I am trying not to forget."

"It sounds like a serious road you have been down," Bishop Sloan replied. "But, -and I'm not sure why I am called upon to do this, you both have my blessing."

"Bishop Sloan," I said with visible worry, "Am I to understand correctly that I have your permission to propose to Mary Balfour?"

"Yes. You two will need counseling if your brain injury is as it seems, but yes, you can propose."

So, as if I had been planning for this moment my entire life, I held out the box and assumed the position on one knee.

Mary Balfour's eyes widened and her face took on a look of confusion as if to say, 'Here? Now?'

Then, as all men do, I stammered out, "I love you Mary Balfour, and I would love it if you would be my wife?"

The look on Mary Balfour's face was priceless and Bishop Sloan had the good sense to pick up his cell phone and snap a few candid photographs. The ring gleamed in a shaft of light that floated across the room.

"Of course I will be your wife," Mary Balfour confirmed. At which time I stood up and kissed her.

Bishop in the room or not, this moment was ours. We embraced and with terrific satisfaction, professed our love for one another.

"I wondered what that box in your pocket was!" Bishop Sloan finished taking pictures.

"I saw you see me," I stammered. "But, I knew it would happen fast.

"First time for this!" the bishop said with a huge smile.

"My girl is full of firsts," I started. "She was the first to be ordained at McDowell, the Episcopal camp." I secretly knew that her parents were waiting to surprise Mary Balfour at my brother's house, a few short miles away. A first for them, no doubt.

"Thank you Bishop Sloan," I said quickly, "for allowing this to happen in your office." I shook his hand.

"Of course, of course," Sloan and Mary Balfour embraced.

"It is not your average day," Sloan said and smiled.

"Well," I said in earnest. "Best friends, for life. A pretty good day, I would say."

"No," I corrected, again feigning nonchalance. "Getting engaged in the bishop's office? Now that's the best day of my life." For the first time since my accident, relaxation poured down my spine.

Mary Balfour smiled at me and I knew this was real.

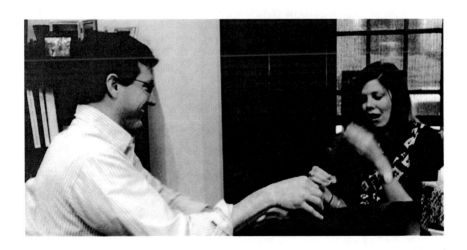

FORCES OF NATURE

BY MURRAY DUNLAP

It came in like a hurricane
Nothing left standing
Just a breeze through my fingers in this shadow of a life
Once lived
But now living again
Nothing is stable
Nothing tied down
Nothing remains, that was
Through forces of nature
A life overturned
But to begin again
Is the freedom of happiness

MURRAY DUNLAP

AUTHOR'S NOTE
"FROM PAIN AND SUFFERING TO JOY"

TO SAY I KNOW PAIN AND SUFFERING might be an understatement. As many people know, I was in a car wreck that put me in a coma for three months. Then I lived out of a wheelchair for six. Then I used a walker for about six more. My memory of this timeline and dates is sketchy at best. I have amnesia and a traumatic brain injury. Memory is no longer my strong-suit. As a full time writer, this disadvantage is maddening. But, I type on.

I had been given much, much physical therapy in order to walk again. I went to multiple therapists to improve my memory and pull myself out of depression. I have joined several gyms to lose the weight I gained in my wheelchair / walker days. Yes, fifty pounds. I published my first book, but having written it before the accident, I had trouble being proud. I did not remember writing it. The interviews and news felt false. I felt as if I was an impostor. The countless hours of therapy aside, my work had been anything but writing.

I had been married at the time of the wreck. A dear girl, she was overcome with the loss of her younger brother just 6 months before. And then her husband of five years underwent profound changes, and no longer resembled the man she had once loved. While I can understand now, at the time I was as confused as a human being can be. I suffered that trauma and loss. But, I brushed myself off and moved.

I was forced to relearn to walk, to drive, and to stop speaking with a slur and crooked eyebrows, and the worst thing (to me personally), a smile that drooped on one side of my mouth.

In the background of this mess, my sister-in-law had gone to Sawyerville Day Camp with Mary Balfour Van Zandt and told her my story. Mary Balfour had thought, he sounds interesting, but a married man. Then, in short order, I was not. And so began the phone calls and emails that led to plane flights and long car rides.

Through all of this, I have started writing again.

A fellow survivor, Kara Swanson, who writes an inspirational blog for brain injury survivors (her injury was in 1996) says, "The curious thing about the auto accident that ended my life was that I lived through it." I add to Kara's sage note -- just like that, my original plan for life vanished. But, as one life ended for me, a better and more fulfilling life began. Thank you Ed. Ed is the man who ran a red light.

As you now know, I have become engaged to the beautiful Mary Balfour Van Zandt. From the very deepest, suicidal despair, to the glorious joy of true love, my life has started making sense again. I had lost track of God and resented my arduous journey, but I have learned that the wreck was not God's plan, but my recovery and meeting the love of my life was.

So I live a profoundly blessed life. The journey from a fat, brain-injured fool in a wheelchair to a life as a published writer who has found love has been, at times, maddening, but the final result is beautiful. Please know that my life is far from perfect, but the pain and suffering brought me here, and give me greater appreciation of the joy.

Murray Dunlap has been published in more than 50 periodicals among which are The Bark Magazine, Virginia Quarterly Review, and Post Road... His first book, Bastard Blue, was published by Press 53 on 6/7/11 (The three year anniversary of a car wreck that almost killed him). It is also a collection of short stories, all fiction.

CPSIA information can be obtained at www.ICGtesting.com
Printed in the USA
LVOW06s1616240715

447498LV00002B/4/P